BAND-AIDS,

BULLETS

and

BOOZE

by
Joan Brady, RN, BSN

Edited by Mary Ann Liotta, RN

Cover Design by Thomas Taylor of Thomcatt Graphics

Vista Publishing, Inc.
473 Broadway
Long Branch, New Jersey 07740
(908) 229-6500

This publication is designed for the reading pleasure of the general public. All characters, places and situations are fictional and are in no way intended to depict actual people, places, or situations.

Printed and bound in the United States of America on acid-free paper

ISBN: 1-880254-15-8

Library of Congress Catalog Card Number 93-94346

U.S.A. Price $14.95
Canada Price $19.95

DEDICATION

To Nurses and Cops everywhere,
whose good deeds and altruistic intentions, so often go unnoticed.

And to my four police officer brothers,

Tom

Paul

Bo

Ed

who so proudly protect and serve.

MEET THE AUTHOR

Joan Brady, RN, BSN has twenty two years of nursing experience. She is a 1972 graduate of William Paterson College (New Jersey), where she received her BSN. In addition to extensive experience in pediatrics, orthopedics, adolescent medicine and nursing management, Joan worked for over seven years as a traveling nurse. Her travels have taken her to hospitals in Pennsylvania, Florida, California, Connecticut, Louisiana, and South Carolina. Her assignments expanded her professional practice to include such specialty areas as renal transplants, vascular surgery, head and neck surgery, urology, pediatric rehabilitation, neurology, and neuro-surgery.

Joan has appeared on several television shows and given numerous radio interviews. In addition to contributing chapters to an orthopedic nursing text book, she has authored many articles on issues that affect nurses both personally and professionally. In her novel, *Fluff My Pillow, Bend My Straw: The Evolution and Undoing of a Nurse*, Joan captured the heart and passion of the nursing profession, giving nurses everywhere an opportunity to remember the "realities" of their first work experiences. However, most important, she gave them the keys to empowerment.

Joan is currently living and working as a per diem staff nurse in her home state of New Jersey. She enjoys spending time with her family and friends, and spending her quiet times working on her next novel.

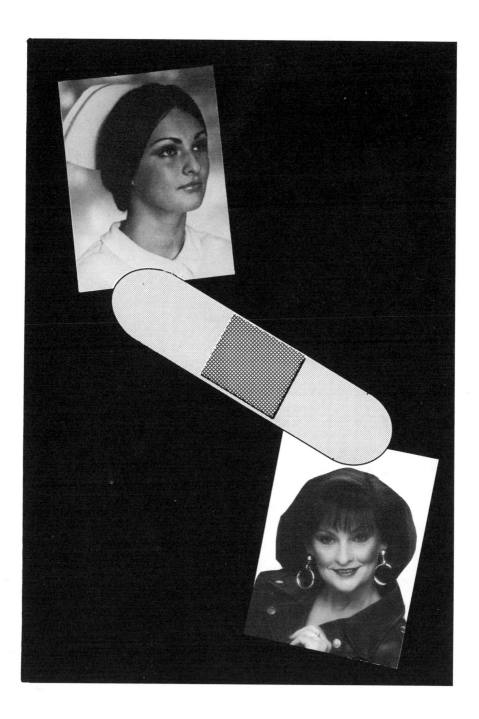

CONTENTS

Page

Prologue

These things only happened to other people. Courtney Quinn never dreamed it would happen to her. She had been a nurse for three years now and she was no stranger to disaster . . . other people's disasters. She still could not conceive of herself as a widow. She even hated the sound of that word. It sounded old. And it sounded lonely. And you weren't supposed to be either of those things when you were twenty-six. What were the chances of this happening, she wondered as she looked out over the sea of blue uniforms before her. She knew she was taking a chance when she married a police officer, but she never expected to lose. Neither does any gambler, she supposed, but marriage itself, was a fifty/fifty risk today. And she and Paul had beat the odds in that category. They had had a wonderful marriage.

The honor guard lifted the flag from Paul's coffin and folded it with military precision. Frank Dooley, Paul's former partner, turned on his heel in military fashion and approached Courtney. His posture was rigid and soldierly, but he didn't try to camouflage the un-soldierly tears.

Poor Frank. He was almost as much a widow as Courtney. It is common knowledge in the brotherhood of police work that a cop has to get along with his partner every bit as well as the person he's going to marry. Their relationship is that important. Their very lives depend on it. Paul had often remarked about his excellent luck in having the best wife and the best partner a man could ask for. After that, and the fact that he was in excellent health, a man couldn't ask for much more, he would say.

Much to most people's surprise, nurses and cops make excellent marriage partners. They are both public servants. Both professions demand a cool head in an emergency and a kind heart. Not to mention the rotating shifts and working weekends and holidays while the rest of the world is at play. People always seem to expect nurses to marry doctors, but Courtney Quinn wouldn't have traded her cop-husband for a dozen doctors.

Suddenly she was overwhelmed with sorrow for her slain husband. Frank said it had been a "routine domestic dispute" when they got the call. He said they almost didn't answer it when they heard the address. They knew it well. They got called there at least once a week, usually on Friday nights. The husband would get his paycheck and go out and get drunk. Then he'd come home and beat up his wife. She would call the police, terrified that her husband would kill her. But without exception, as soon as Paul and Frank restrained the husband and cuffed him, the wife would start pleading with them to let him go. She refused to press charges. She made it difficult to take her calls seriously.

But that night would not be routine, How could they have known the husband would have a gun this time? Paul had tried to talk the man into dropping the gun, but there was no reasoning with him. Both Paul and Frank had stood in the doorway, trying to calm the frenzied drunk. Neither had reached for his gun before entering and it was too late now. Any sudden movement on their part could cost either one of them their lives. Frank said Paul had been valiant. When he saw the twitch of the man's trigger finger, be put his left arm across his chest, as they had been taught in the police academy, and drew his gun with his dominant hand. But he was too late. He never had a chance. Unless you count the fifty/fifty chance he had of the drunk choosing to shoot Frank instead.

The left arm across the chest was to possibly take the bullet in the arm and hopefully deflect it from the direction of the heart and other vital organs. Obviously, it didn't always work. Frank had said that this domestic dispute was at the end of their tour of duty and both men had just removed their bulky and uncomfortable bullet proof vests. Since they knew the address well and felt comfortable that they were in no imminent danger, They hadn't taken the time to don the bullet proof vests again. Frank and Paul had gone through the Academy together and Frank was embarrassed to admit that one of the first lessons they had learned was that the most dangerous call for a police officer, surprisingly, is a domestic disturbance.

Courtney thought back to that devastating night, the one that had changed her life forever. She wondered what Paul's last thoughts were. It hurt to be left out of something as important as that. They had shared everything, the good feelings and the bad. She was his wife. She had a right to know. But fate is not fair . . . reasonable or predictable. All she could do was hope that it didn't hurt very much. And that the paramedics had been kind to him.

Frank Dooley was holding the folded flag in trembling hands as he made his way to present it to Courtney. This was the part she had seen a million times on T.V. dramas, and a million times this was the part that made her cry. But not this time. Perhaps she was too numb to cry. Perhaps she was still in shock. She had such a bizarre thought as she put her hands out to accept the flag. She was thinking, so this is how Jackie Kennedy did it. This must be how she conducted herself so courageously at President Kennedy's funeral. She probably felt just like this. Anesthetized with shock. Oddly enough, it wasn't anything like Courtney expected it to be. Always the nurse, she marveled at the human mind's capacity to protect itself from pain. Paul would have laughed.

Someone was taking her by the arm and leading her away from the grave site. It was Frank Dooley, guiding and comforting his partner's widow, just as he and his partner had promised they would do for one another. But neither man had believed for an instant that either of them would die of anything but old age. How wrong they had been.

"Hang on, Babe" Frank whispered as he squeezed Courtney's arm and led her to the black limousine that stood waiting for her.

That was all it took. Courtney felt a giant sob escape from her lungs before she could put a stop to it. Her entire being quivered with pain from the very root of her soul. Giant tears pooled in her blue eyes, then spilled onto the chiseled face that Paul had loved. The face he used to kiss. The face he would never see again.

Chapter One

Starting Over

Courtney Quinn looked up from the "Classifieds" of yesterdays' newspaper. She hadn't had the energy to go out and buy today's paper. In fact, she'd hadn't had the energy to do much of anything these days. Her heart just wasn't in anything she did or didn't do. How could it be? It was still broken. Still trying to heal from the irreparable damage done to it, because some drunk with a gun had shot her brave and devoted husband. Paul had just been doing his job. He and his partner, Frank Dooley, had just been trying to protect the somewhat masochistic wife of a slimeball. Courtney recognized that she was being bitter and perhaps unfair to the woman who had called Paul and Frank for help. But she had lost her precious husband because of it.

She looked around the living room with tear-filled eyes. It was easier to look around when the vision of "their" things was blurred by tears. It somehow made the pain less sharp. She gazed at the array of pictures across the mantle. Pictures of their wedding. Pictures of her and Paul on a boat in the Cayman Islands, where they had honeymooned. They were both tanned and smiling in the picture, completely unsuspecting of the tragedy that lay only three years in their future.

As if sensing her pain, Zachary, the Bassett Hound puppy that Paul had fallen in love with three years earlier, nuzzled up under Courtney's arm. He settled down across the unread classified ads in the newspaper as if asking her not to do what she knew had to be done.

"Zachary, we can't stay here forever" she said painfully as she stroked the dog's thick fur. Zachary looked at her with big, sad eyes and tilted his head as if to ask "Why not?'

"Because, we've got to start over again. Without Paul."

Zachary stared his disagreement at her.

"Paul would have wanted it that way for us" she added.

Zachary put his big, droopy head down on her lap and Courtney managed to turn the page of the classifieds to the section for nurses. She never thought she'd ever be doing this. She had thought her life was set, once she had fallen in love with Paul. She had made the old female mistake she supposed, of assuming everything would be all right, now that she had found the man she wanted to spend the rest of her life with.

She thought back to when she had first met him. She was a disillusioned and disenchanted nurse at the time, working on a hectic Med/Surg floor in one of Philadelphia's busiest trauma centers. She was just out of school and had had so much to learn. She was also naively caught up in a love affair at the time, with a handsome, yet shallow, worldly, yet egotistical OB/GYN resident. Paul had been working undercover at the time, quarding police who were patients and protecting police informants. And unbeknown to Courtney, he was also working on unraveling a case of administrative embezzlement. Paul have been a knight in shining armor as he helped her to see that she was investing too much of herself into her job. That she was being taken advantage of. He had applauded, while most others had criticized, her attempt to embarrass the hospital administration by transferring to the Housekeeping Department. He had been in love with her all along. And he had waited patiently for her to find out for herself that the romance with her commitment-shy, doctor boyfriend, would be her demise. He had been there to pick up the pieces when it all had fallen apart. He had been her best friend, her hero, her mentor . . . and finally, her love.

He had encouraged her to assert herself against the hospital administrators who were taking her and countless other nurses for granted. He had even helped her to get the much needed publicity that had been so effective in making and embarrassing spectacle out of the hospital administrators. It was Paul who had supported her and encouraged her to go on the T.V. talk show circuit, speaking out for nurses and starting a new career for herself. A career she might not have had the confidence to pursue if not for his unwavering support. He believed in her conviction that nurses should no longer play the role of mindless little handmaids to the doctors. That nurses are professionals and should finally be treated as such, both in terms of financial compensation and in terms of respect. He had never experienced a moment of jealousy for his much sought-after and popular wife. He had been nothing but proud of her and her accomplishments

But now he was gone. Forever. And no amount of tears or regret, or **anything** would ever bring him back. She cradled Zachary in her arms, wishing it were Paul, and Zach looked up at her with big understanding eyes.

She looked through the classifieds. Even though Paul had had the foresight to take care of her in the possibility of this kind of tragedy, she still wanted to work. It would be good for her to have some kind of a routine again. She still did a lot of talks for nursing organizations and nursing schools, encouraging nurses to stand up for the respect they deserved. And she still occasionally appeared on talk shows and was in the process of writing a book on her philosophy of nursing. But it wasn't enough to fill the terrible, empty void that Paul's death had left in her life.

An ad for Emergency Room nurse in Atlantic City's "City Hospital" caught her eye. Courtney had never worked the Emergency Room, except when she was a student nurse, but the ad said they would give "on the job training". Courtney knew that she needed something challenging and rewarding to take her outside of herself and her sorrow. The Emergency Room might be a very good place to start. It struck her as the next logical step to take in her battle to forget. In the battle to find a life for herself again.

She liked the idea of Atlantic City. It seemed as good a place as any to start rebuilding a life. It had been six long and lonely months since Paul's untimely death. And though she thrived on the support of her friends and relatives, she was slightly overdosed on the sympathetic looks and aching for her that she saw mirrored in other people's eyes. She needed to leave Philadelphia, at least for a while. There had been too many happy times here with Paul and she would never get on with her life as long as she was reminded daily of the happiness that had been so cruelly and suddenly snatched away from her.

She could guess what they would all say when they heard this plan. "What will you do there? Wouldn't you rather be among friends and family who love you? Who understand what you're going through?" But that was exactly what she needed to get away from now. As long as the sympathy lasted, the pain and reminders would last. No, she needed a change. She needed a routine and a purpose. She couldn't spend her days just hanging around anymore, missing Paul and knowing that she had lost something that could never, ever be replaced. Besides, Paul would have been the first to encourage her to take a chance. He always had.

The more she thought about it, the better Atlantic City sounded. It was close enough to Philadelphia so that she could still be near friends and family, just not as often. And many Philadelphians spent their summers at the "Jersey Shore" anyway. In a way, it would be a little like home away from home, she supposed. And besides, the night life was one of a kind. There were great shows available with terrific entertainment. And there were always the casinos and the slot machines. The place was filled with flashing lights and ringing bells and nothing to think about but getting three triple bars or four of a kind or royal flushes. It was an easy place to lose yourself and your problems. And that's exactly what Courtney Quinn was looking to do.

For the first time in months, she had the energy to do something constructive. She began to write her resume, careful to include her experience as a 3 to 11 charge Nurse on a busy, sixty bed Med/Surg Unit in Center City, Philadelphia. She was also careful to omit her short lived career in the Housekeeping Department. No matter how much she had criticized nursing, she had to admit it was comforting to know you could always come back to it. And that was more than you could say for a lot of professions.

Courtney looked around the little townhouse in which she and Paul had shared three such happy years. She knew she would now have to start the painful task of selling it and even worse, of packing all their things and reliving memories, one more time. She looked down at Zachary still curled in her lap and rumpled the thick fur on his neck, the way Paul used to tease him. Zachary looked up at her with a longing in his eyes that Courtney completely understood.

"Don't worry Zach" she murmured. "I'll take good care of us. You'll like Atlantic City, I promise."

Chapter Two

Nine-One-One

Nine-One-One was the name of a tavern located on a small side street right along Atlantic City's famous boardwalk. Actually, it was more of an alley than a side street. And actually, the name wasn't really Nine-One-One. That was the street address, but since the tavern was frequented mostly by off-duty cops and off-duty nurses and doctors from the big city hospital across the street, it needed no gimmicky name. Nine-One-One said it all.

The cops were known to stop in, particularly after the 4 to 12 tour of duty was finished, but they also had no aversion to patronizing the place at eight o'clock in the morning when they rotated shifts. The nurses showed up mostly at 12 midnight, after finishing up 3 to 11 shift, but they were also known to stop in on occasion at eight in the morning, especially if they'd had to work a double shift. It was nice to share war stories or to hear of someone who may have had a worse night than you did . . . if that were possible. The interns and residents seemed to have the most random schedules. They would stop in during a lull in the action on their nights on-call in City Hospital's Emergency Room. Often they drank just coffee or club soda, in case they had to suddenly go running back. Sometimes, they didn't care. And neither did anybody else. There was a kind of camaraderie among the group that frequented Nine-One-One. Everyone respected everyone else's right to do whatever they had to do to get through the day - or night - whatever the case may be. Whatever the shift may be.

There had never been any reason to name the place, even though it's location was almost impossible for an outsider to find. And the seasoned cops and City Hospital's Emergency Room workers liked it that way. It left little chance of some goodie-two-shoes tourist or some local-do-gooder, overhearing the cynical and sometimes graphic conversations that went on in there. It was a place where a "public servant" could throw down a few cold brewskies and be completely her or himself, without fear of horrifying the public. Or of being "reported".

The place was well known only to the people who needed to know it. And the patrons eventually got to know one another. Cops were frequently visiting City Hospital's Emergency Room, either as patients themselves, or bringing someone in who was in dire need of medical attention. A kind of brotherhood had developed among the patrons of Nine-One-One, and it was an unspoken rule that cops never gave nurses and doctors tickets . . . and cops never waited in line in the Emergency Room, no matter how trivial the injury.

The owner, Sam Manetti, and his bartenders were only too happy to have a constant crowd of cops around, since Nine-One-One was located in a pretty rough section of town. It also didn't hurt to befriend people who were experts at CPR, and who could get you in ahead of the usual two to three hour wait to be seen in City Hospital's ER. Not to mention all the free legal and medical advice floating around a place like that.

To show his appreciation for their patronage, Sam Manetti always saw to it that a bottle of "Irish Mist" was kept on top of the coffee urn in the back room. It was there just in case the cops (or anyone else, for that matter) wanted to put a little "life" into their coffee before venturing out into the damp, cold winters of Atlantic City. Sam also made sure that all his people knew to give a key to one of the rooms upstairs to any of the patrons who'd had too much to drink and needed a place to sleep it off, rather than drive home intoxicated. All things considered, it was a mutually advantageous arrangement for all involved. Or, as some of the medical people called it, a "symbiotic" relationship, whatever that meant.

But Sam was used to the medical people always throwing around the big words. At first he had thought they were just showing off, but slowly, he realized that they really couldn't help themselves. They truly spoke a different language. He called it "Doctor-ese", even though the nurses spoke it just as fluently.

Nine-One-One was a homey little place. Nothing fancy. And that's just the way they all liked it. It was dimly lit by fake Tiffany lamps, which, coupled with the haze that settled over a person after a few beers or whatever, was very flattering to even the most homely face. Best of all, it was small and well heated in the winter. In the summer, Sam kept it cool with ceiling fans that swirled the dank, salty ocean air in circles around the bar, as patrons drank beer from frosted mugs. The only even slightly difficult season was "Hurricane Season", usually in September, and even that really wasn't so bad.

It's just that every now and then, when the mighty and moody Atlantic Ocean decided to kick up, it would sometimes flood the floor of the tavern. Usually it only happened during the fierce hurricanes that were known to slam into the city, which was really an island, a little known fact. But sometimes even a good, "Nor'easter" could be strong enough to bring the ocean waters flirting at the edge of the doorway and gradually saturate the floor from all directions. But, it too, added a sort of charm to the place. Customers who came in before the tide did, found they had to stay on their barstools till the tide went out. Not that anyone really minded, or even noticed for that matter. And there was never anything valuable enough to get upset about damaging. All in all, the place, like most of the people in it, was legendary.

And speaking of legends, there was one patron, who fit all categories of patrons without being a doctor, nurse or cop. He was a Roman Catholic priest. Father Murphy. He was not only the Hospital Chaplain and occupied a special place in the hearts of the hospital personnel, he was also the official chaplain for Atlantic City's police department and held a special place in their hearts as well. To say nothing of the special stool he occupied at Nine-One-One. He was often called to the hospital to comfort a grieving family or to administer Last Rites to the dying. He was also very often called upon to ride in a squad car with the officers to try to talk someone out of a suicide attempt or to administer Last Rites . . . depending on how well the "Don't commit suicide" talk went. He was well known to everyone in Nine-One-One, and was even known to have heard an unsolicited confession or two right at the bar. You had to like the guy.

Next to Father Murphy, usually sat a somewhat burned-out, veteran member of the police department, Mike Murphy, no relation to the good Father. Mike Murphy had put in twenty-two years with the department and spent all twenty-two of those years as a patrolman. He didn't want the promotions offered to him. In fact, he never even took the Sergeant's Test or any of a number of roads that would have helped him climb the ladder. "The ladder to what?" he would say. "If there's a pot of gold waiting for me up there, I'd go for it - maybe. But given my druthers, I'd just as soon stay out on the streets. That's where I like it". No one ever argued with him. They didn't have the nerve. Mike Murphy could be a mean drunk. In fact, it was said that that was how he'd lost his wife and family. He never talked about it much, unless he was drunk. Apparently his wife had left him with their four kids eight years ago, because Mike couldn't give up the bottle. And though he talked big, no one ever really saw Mike Murphy make a pass at another woman. It was common knowledge that he was still in love with his wife and that he missed his kids terribly. Just not enough to give up drinking. He was mean and sarcastic to everyone, especially his rookie partner, who it was said, would rather take his chances with the scum on the streets, than risk spending eight hours in a patrol car with Mike Murphy. The only one anyone had ever seen Mike respect to was "The Padre", as they called him. Father Murphy.

Fred Gantz was the poor, unfortunate rookie, who had had the dreadful luck of getting Mike Murphy for his partner. Fred had always thought that if he showed enough kindness and perhaps tolerance of Mike Murphy's sarcastic ways, perhaps they could one day be friends. And besides, Fred was certain that he could learn a lot from a veteran like Mike.

Right from the start, Mike had made it difficult for Fred to be tolerant of his new partner. For one thing, even though he was only twenty-seven, Fred was losing his hair at an alarming rate and he tried desperately any kind of remedy or new hairstyle that would improve or hide his disappearing hairline. Once Fred had come to work with a new "perm" that he confidently thought camouflaged his vanishing tresses. Admittedly, the hairstyle had been a little extreme and so Mike Murphy had dubbed him "Howitzer Head Fred". In the same breath, Mike had also offered to give him a "hair graft" from his very hairy and virile looking back. This had amused the entire group at Roll Call that day, and Fred had been mortified. Worse yet, the nickname stuck.

Next to "Howitzer Head Fred" usually sat Dorothey McFadden, one of the City Hospital's finest Emergency Room nurses. It was agreed by most of the cops, that if they ever had the terrible misfortune of sustaining a serious injury, they'd much rather look up and see Dorothy McFadden stand-in there, than **any** doctor. She was **that** good.

"So what, Dot" they called her. She had earned the name by more years than anyone wanted to count, working with the drunks, pimps, hookers and criminals across the street in the Emergency Room. And though she was a regular customer at Nine-One-One, she was known for being exceptionally cool under pressure. Any kind of pressure. She was known to have acquired this unflappable attitude by preceding every call for help and every announcement of disaster, by snarling in a truly disgusted tone, **"SO WHAT?"** Then she would gather whatever equipment she and the doctors would need and get to work with the competence of a brain surgeon and the grace of a ballerina. Many a senior resident or lowly intern freely admitted that they would not be what they were today, if it had not been for the excellent emergency skills they had learned from "So What, Dot".

Next to So What, Dot usually sat whichever interns or residents were on-call that night, soaking up free and valid medical advice from the master.

The southwest corner of the tavern was unofficially reserved for a cop named Frank Stoner. Frank was a "K-9" cop, the ones who ride around with a well trained police dog for a partner. This was a good thing in Frank Stoner's case, since he didn't relate very well to people. He never sat at the bar among his comrades. He just came in and sat down at a little table in the southwest corner of the tavern, always ordering two beers, one for himself and one for "Boris", his Rotweiler partner. He had rarely been known to spring for a round of drinks for his brother police officers. In fact, the occasions on which he'd bought anyone but himself and Boris a round, were so rare that the other patrons of the bar began a tradition of carving a notch in the old wooden wall behind Frank's table for each round he' bought. So far, in the six years that he'd been on the force, there were only seven notches behind his table.

Boris sat loyally at his master's side, ever alert . . . that is at least until after his second beer. Then his big, perceptive eyes would begin to get a little hazy and droop. After the third beer, Boris's whole body would begin to droop and he would settle down on the floor at his master's feet and sleep, keeping one ear only, perked and ready to respond.

Frank believed in sharing **everything** with his dog. There were stories about his girlfriend to that effect, purely hearsay, of course. Boris would always join his partner Frank, in a few "Brewskies" after work, but even the brewskies did nothing to loosen the tongue of Frank Stoner. "Stoner the Loner" they all called him.

And then there was the story of the night that Boris had pranced up to the bar with a five dollar bill in his powerful jaws and laid it on the bar, a trick "Stone the Loner" had worked hard with him to perfect. Stoner still hadn't figured out a way to train Boris to carry the beers back to their table. But he needn't have worried that night. Mike Murphy had been so impressed with Boris's "buying" a round, that he'd carried the beers back for him and carved a notch in the wall above Boris's usual station. It was said that if Boris had pockets, Stoner probably never even would have bought **him** a round.

All in all, Nine-One-One was a one of a kind place. If the walls could talk, it was commonly agreed that they would be booked on every talk show in existence.

Chapter Three

The Otis Elevator Procedure

The newspaper lied. Or the hospital did. In all likelihood, Courtney Quinn had to admit that it had probably been the hospital. They had promised "on the job training" for new Emergency Room nurses. But they had never mentioned that their idea of on the job training was to throw you in cold on a night when another more experienced nurse was working. This way, you could bellow questions out to her as you whizzed past each other, running from cubicle to cubicle, trying to determine who was in the most urgent need of care. When was she going to learn not to bite, every time a hospital threw a piece of bait? Nothing had changed much, if at all, since three years ago when Courtney had first stated speaking out about just such horrendous injustices.

Well at least the time flew fast in the Emergency Room and shifts were over before you knew it. Courtney was just thinking that there was only a hour left of her shift with Dorothy McFadden, otherwise known as "So What, Dot". She knew she was over the hump. Anything critical that could happen, Dorothy would show her how to handle. She was a bit of a rough and cynical character, but she was one terrific ER nurse . . . and she knew it.

Just then, the doors burst open and a patient was wheeled in by the local first aid. No one, besides the patient and her anxious looking daughter looked too alarmed.

"What have we got here?" So What, Dot asked calmly, already having assessed the situation thoroughly enough to know that it was nothing life threatening. Courtney envied her for that skill and couldn't wait till the day **she** could look at a terrified-looking patient and family and infect them with the calm reassurance of an expert.

"Looks like a dislocated total hip" the paramedic said indifferently. "You got any coffee?" he asked, with a bit more enthusiasm.

Dot pointed the way to the fresh pot of coffee that sat on the table in the back room and asked the family what had happened. The family, described in too much detail and with too much emotion for Dot's taste, that "Mother" had had a Total Hip Replacement six weeks ago and that today she had tripped on a throw rug and couldn't get up. That was all the information Dot needed at this point. She pointed to the waiting room and asked the family to wait out there until the orthopedic resident on call examined the patient.

"Why can't they wait in the cubicle with the patient?" Courtney asked in a concerned voice. After all, the patient looked like she was in a great deal of pain and what harm would it do to let her family be with her to comfort her?

"Because families get on my nerves" said So What, Dot, reading Courtney's naive and innocent mind. "C'mon, you wanna learn something? Ordinarily I'd let her wait awhile. A dislocated Total Hip isn't exactly a life threatening emergency, but since you're new and you got a lot to learn, you might as well start now. Come with me," Dot said as she led Courtney toward the cubicle where the orderly had deposited the patient.

"What do you know about Total Hip Replacements?" So What, Dot asked as she led the way.

"Well, I know the hip is a ball and socket joint and since it bears so much weight, when it becomes severely arthritic or badly fractured, they just remove the whole joint and put in an entirely new one." Courtney was finally grateful for all the "overflow" Orthopedic patients she had grudgingly accepted during her days on 6-South in Philadelphia.

"That's right. What else?" So What, Dot, persisted. "What's the biggest danger of a Total Hip Replacement? I mean after the initial recovery time in the hospital."

Courtney wasn't really sure about this. "Dislocation?" she guessed.

"Very good, Quinn. And how do you know when a hip is dislocated? What kinds of things do you look for?"

"Pain?" Courtney was guessing.

"Yeah, but that doesn't really tell you anything. Every patient in this place will tell you they're in pain. That doesn't mean they all have dislocated Total Hips. Come on. Think."

Courtney drew a blank.

"The leg is usually shorter than the other one" Dot answered for her. "And usually it's rotated at an odd angle, which makes sense, since the ball is no longer in the socket. What else?" she continued to question Courtney.

"I don't know" Courtney answered honestly.

They had reached the patient's bedside at that point and So What, Dot drew the curtains around the patient. She didn't do it as much for the patient's privacy as she did so that everyone else would leave her alone while she was busy with this old patient and this novice nurse.

She pulled the sheet up from the patient's feet to her waist, never making eye contact. She introduced herself and gave the usual speech about how she would be the woman's nurse. It was a speech she must have given a million times in her her eighteen year career in City Hospital's Emergency Room.

As predicted, yet much to Courtney's awere, the patient's left leg appeared markedly shorter than the right and the foot was rotated at an awkward, outward angle.

"Another way of being fairly certain, before the x-ray, is that if you lift the leg slightly and try to gently rotate it, you'll find it has little or no range of motion and usually causes the patient a great deal of pain. So What, Dot demonstrated this as the woman grimaced in pain and pleaded to see her doctor.

"Now the most painful part of this problem is going to be when we call the doctor" Dot said, lowering the dislocated limb.

"You mean the Orthopedic Resident?" Courtney asked.

"Well, him too. But unfortunately, we're going to have to all Arnie Weissberg too, you know, the private attending physician."

Courtney knew this conversation should be held out of earshot of the patient, but she had so much to learn and she wasn't about to interrupt the master. She didn't know how often she would get the opportunity in the future to get this kind of information, right from the horse's mouth. "I don't understand" Courtney questioned. "Why should Dr. Weissberg be mad if he has to come in? It's his night on call for the ER, isn't it? And besides, I thought we just had to call the Ortho resident and let **him** call the attending, no?"

"Well, technically you're right, but you see, it's too close to July and the residents are still pretty green. It's gonna take the new Ortho resident a little more time to figure out what's wrong. And I saw Dr. Weissberg on his way out the door earlier. He told me he knew he was taking a chance, but he and his wife made plans for dinner and a show and he really didn't want to be interrupted. I think it's their anniversary or something. He's a nice guy, but he can really fly off the handle when things don't go his way. Trust me, he's not gonna like this."

"I still don't understand why **we** have to notify him" Courtney stated again, feeling a bit like the old handmaiden role.

So What, Dot laughed. "Believe me, it's for the patient's sake. By the time we get an Operating Room ready for her and the on-call team called in, Arnie and his wife will be in bed. I'm not saying what they'll be doing there, but I guarantee he'll be less ornery if he knows ahead of time that he's gonna have to spend his anniversary night in the OR."

"I thought sometimes, they gave I.V. valium right here in the ER and tried to reduce the dislocation here at the beside." Courtney was beginning to remember what her year on 6-South had taught her.

"Good point" Dot said with a knowing smile, "but trust me. I been here a long time. She's the type that will end up in the OR I hope not, for her sake and for Arnie Weissberg's sake. If they can get the hip back in down here, great. Arnie can tell the wife to keep the champagne on ice. But my money says they'll be spending the night in the OR."

Courtney correctly quessed that there were just some things that could not be taught. They had to be experienced. And they had something to do with instincts. She marveled at Dot's allotment of both.

Dot interrupted Courtney's thoughts at that point. "Listen, make sure you keep her NPO - nothing, not even water by mouth. The Ortho resident probably doesn't realize it yet that she's going to the OR tonight, but you let him know. He should be on his way down. Meanwhile, I'll make the supreme

11

sacrifice of giving Arnie the bad news. Wish me luck." And with that she walked off toward the ward secretary to look up Dr. Weissberg's beeper number.

Dot had been right. The Ortho resident had done everything Dot had done to make the diagnosis and had come to the same conclusion. Arnie Weissberg came stalking through the Emergency Room twenty minutes after receiving the call. And though he was dressed in a suit and tie, he quickly changed to OR greens and began trying to salvage the rest of his night by trying to force an unyielding stainless steel femoral head into the acetabular component. The valium flowed and though the patient was experiencing discomfort, she didn't seem to mind. Finally, sweating and breathing hard, Dr. Weissberg surrendered to the stubborn hip and told the resident to notify the OR that they were coming up.

The OR had been hopping that night and it was going to take them awhile to accommodate this non-emergent patient. Dr. Weissberg paced the floor and made several phone calls to his disappointed, yet optimistic wife. She kept promising to wait up for him, but as the time ticked by, and still no OR could take them, she became less and less interested in waiting up for their romantic evening together.

Finally the OR was ready and the doctors went up to scrub. At the same time, the orderlies in the ER were suddenly hit with an influx of new patients and nobody seemed to have time to transport the patient up to the waiting hands and equipment of Dr. Weissberg. He must have called the ER secretary five times in five minutes ranting and raving about the inefficiency of this place. After all, his patient had a dislocated hip and hopefully, he still had a bottle of champagne on ice, waiting for him at home.

By the time one of the orderlies found the time to take the extremely patient woman to the Operating Room, she smiled sweetly at him and asked, "Is Dr. Weissberg going to fix my hip now?"

"Yes" smiled the orderly. "And you have been a patient, patient" he laughed. Then he added, more to himself than to anyone else, "I guess that's why they call you patients".

It was a known fact that the elevators in this portion of the hospital were antiques. Some said they'd been there since the year of the flood. The point was, that the elevators were not known for their efficiency and it was rumored that Dr. Weissberg had called three more times while the poor orderly was trying to get the equipment-laden bed onto the elevator. As was often the case, the elevator car didn't stop evenly with the floor and the orderly had to push with all his might to get the traction laden bed onto the elevator. He took a few deep breaths then gave it everything he had, ramming the bed onto the elevator. The patient let out a shriek as the bed bounced over a bump and slammed into the back wall of the elevator car.

"I'm sorry, Ma'am, I'm really sorry" the horrified orderly apologized. "Did I hurt you?" he asked, already knowing the answer.

"Well, you know something?" the woman began through her valium haze as she began to rub her formerly painful hip. I think I feel better. My hip doesn't hurt nearly as much. I think it's better now."

The orderly figured it was just the effect of the drugs, but he was just as glad the woman wasn't mad at him and now probably wouldn't tell anyone of his forceful entry into the elevator.

When Dr. Weissberg examined the woman's hip in the OR, before sliding her over onto the table, he couldn't help but notice that both legs were of equal length now and the left foot was no longer rotated at an irregular angle. He didn't understand it, but the woman kept saying something about how much better she felt ever since that nice young man had pushed her over the bump in the elevator. Dr. Weissberg and his resident stared at each other in utter confusion, but ordered an x-ray anyway.

The x-ray showed a perfectly positioned Total hip and the patient was more comfortable than she'd been since the fall. It was determined that the jolt of going over such a big bump in the elevator had popped the hip back into place. It was then dubbed the "Otis Elevator Procedure" for dislocated hips.

And best of all, the ice wasn't even melted when Dr. Weissberg got home to his waiting wife later that evening.

"I don't know about you, but I'm ready for a drink," So What, Dot announced, as she and Courtney cleaned up after themselves and gave report to the next shift.

"Sounds good to me" Courtney answered. The truth was, **anything** but going home, would have sounded good to her these days. The nights were always the hardest. That's why working the 3 to 11 shift was so good for her. And going out for a drink after work was like an added bonus. It helped to anesthetize her further. So far, she hadn't mentioned her tragic past to anyone. It still hurt too much to talk about it. And besides, she didn't want any more sympathy. She wanted a life and a new beginning and maybe even a few good laughs. And she knew that those things would be extremely limited to her is she ever let anyone know what she was going through. "Where do people go for a drink around here?" she heard herself ask.

"Nine-One-One" So What, Dot answered.

"Is it **that** much of an emergency?" Courtney asked.

Dot laughed. It was a friendly and warm and very welcomed laugh. "No" she said. "It's a place where everyone hangs out after work. It's mostly people from our ER and a bunch of cops who hang out there." Dot didn't miss Courtney's face suddenly drop and her creamy complexion go pale at the mention of cops. "You're not in some kind of trouble with the law" she probed, unsure of exactly who this new, but very likable, Courtney Quinn character was. She saw great potential in this new, young nurse. She also saw unspeakable sadness behind the blue eyes. And she liked that Courtney had not yet shared any of her personal life with anyone. You could trust a person like that. She'd fit right in at Nine-One-One. Dot was certain of that.

Courtney regained her composure and forced a smile that she really didn't feel. "No, I'm not in trouble with the law" she said softly, almost sadly. She took a deep breath, let it out and added, "in fact I sort of have a soft spot in my heart for cops. Let's go."

Chapter Four

Making Friends

Nine-One-One was fairly crowded that night. By the looks of things, the cops must have had a rough night too. There were two empty seats at the bar when Courtney and So What, Dot made their entrance. The two seats were between Mike Murphy, the twenty two year veteran of the police force, who intensely disliked his new rookie partner, and Joseph James, III, M.D..

Actually Joseph James III, M.D., was really a "Doctor of Osteopathy" or "D.O." as they were called. But he didn't like people to know that if they didn't have to. There wasn't all that much difference between an M.D. and a D.O., except a slightly shorter course of academic training and a slightly different philosophy on healing. The biggest reason that Joseph James, III had become a "D.O." though, was because he had been rejected by the Medical Schools of his choice. He felt he was every bit as well trained as any M.D., and so did a lot of other people. After all, you were allowed to have M.D. license plates on your car if you were a D.O.. And of course, Joseph James, III took full advantage of that little added extra . . . on his red corvette. There was a standard joke around the hospital that said something about "How can you tell when someone is a D.O.?" And the answer, which Joseph James, III did not think was funny was, "By the M.D. tags on his car."

Still though, the title of D.O. didn't hurt him any. People still addressed him as "Doctor" and women found him every bit as appealing as his M.D. counterparts. The only thing that bothered him was that if people got mixed up, as his mother frequently did, and mixed the letter up, he ended up being an "O.D." or "Over Dose," instead of the coveted "D.O.". His mother was very proud of him, but he hated it when she got mixed up and introduced him to her friends, or worse yet, to her friends' daughter as "my son the O.D."

Joseph James, III had an eye for good looking women. Some people like So What, Dot said that was **all** he had for women. But, who cared? What did she know? Well, well. Apparently she knew a rather pretty nurse who looked like the newest addition to Nine-One-One. It could have been the Jack Daniel's, but this new nurse had a knock-out figure and pretty blue eyes. Joseph James, III kept his eye on Courtney Quinn, as he continued his conversation across two barstools with Mike Murphy. He watched Dot guide this new "Honey" to the two stools between him and Mike and figured if he could keep up his conversation with Mike, it would be a great opening to get to know this cute, new honey.

Courtney and So What, Dot settled down on their barstools and each ordered a draft beer in an iced mug. Nice touch for an August night, he thought.

Courtney leaned over and whispered into Dot's ear, "Who's the guy with the white lips?"

It took great control for Dot to keep from aspirating on her cold beer, but she studied Joseph James, III and smiled approvingly at Courtney's astute observation. "That's Joseph James, III, D.O." she whispered. "But he'd rather you not know about the 'D.O.' part yet. He likes people to think he's an M.D.. He's got a real hang-up about it. Truth is, it·doesn't mean anything to anyone but him."

"Why does he have white lips?"

"He's got a nervous stomach. He's always drinking Maalox, especially before morning rounds or when he's moonlighting in the ER." Dot was smirking as she raised her mug to her lips and took a long swallow. "Now ask me what kind of car he drives", she added.

"What kind of car does he drive?" Courtney obediently asked.

"A red Corvette with M.D. license plates."

"You mean he's **impotent**?" Courtney asked with exaggerated wide eyes.

This time, Dot really did aspirate on her beer. When she finally stopped choking and was able to find her voice again, she said "You knew about that too? I thought you were from Philadelphia?"

"I am. So what, Dot?"

Dot laughed again. "You know something, Quinn? You're really all right. I thought that was just a New Jersey joke."

"What? That guys who drive Corvettes, especially red ones, are impotent?" She was laughing now. "That's not a joke" she continued, "It's a well known fact. They have to prove something."

"I know" answered Dot. "That's one of my golden rules. I never date a guy who drives a Corvette. No matter what color it is."

"The guy or the Vette?" Courtney teased.

"Either" came Dot's quick reply.

God, it felt good to laugh. Courtney hadn't felt this silly or had this much fun in a very long time. She thought she'd forgotten how.

Joseph James, III was checking out Courtney as he continued his conversation with Mike Murphy, who was sitting on the other side of So What, Dot. He liked her smile. And her easy laugh, though he had no idea what she had found so funny. He wondered how well Dot knew her and what his chances of being introduced were. Well, he'd give it a shot. Here goes.

"Dot" he called over Courtney's beer, appearing not to notice her. "Mike and I were just talking about recurrent dreams and I was explaining what they teach us in Med. School about stuff like that." There. He had done it. He'd let this adorable little creature know that he was a doctor. "You ever have any dreams like that?" he asked, hoping for a chance to show off.

"Yeah, but maybe I'd better introduce you to my friend here, since we all know that's the **real** reason you're so suddenly interested in my dreams." Dot turned to Courtney and motioned with her mug of beer, "Courtney Quinn, I'd like you to meet Joe James."

Joseph James, III hated it when people introduced him that way. He liked it much better if they used his full name or even "Dr. Joseph James". It sounded so much classier, which is exactly why Dot didn't do it.

Next she raised her mug in Mke Murphy's direction and gave the same speech, only this time introducing Mike as a police officer. Mike nodded his head toward Courtney and Dot mentioned that she was a new ER nurse at City Hospital. Courtney felt the immediate acceptance and camaraderie among the patrons of this place and she liked it.

"So Dot, you were saying . . . " Joseph James, III continued, trying to draw Courtney into some kind of conversation.

"What? About Dreams?" Dot vaguely remembered.

"Yeah. You were going to tell me about any recurrent dreams you might have had, so that maybe I can interpret them for you."

Dot guffawed loudly. "I don't really dream, Doctor" she said sarcastically, "but I have lots of fantasies. Want to hear one?" she said, deliberately baiting him.

"Shoot" he said, in what he hoped was a nonchalant voice.

"O.K. I hope you can handle this" she goaded.

Courtney had no idea what was about to come next.

"Well see, Doctor, sometimes I have this fantasy about being in the Emergency Room . . . "

"Go on" said Dr. James, intrigued.

Dot suppressed a smile and went on. "There's this little old lady who comes in with gastroenteritis. She's also arthritic, and suddenly she tells me she's got to get to a bathroom. I try to get her to use the bedpan, but she refuses. She insists on going into the bathroom, walker and all. It takes her forever to shuffle into the bathroom, then turn around to sit on the toilet." Dot could see the boredom creeping into Joe James' eyes. "Here's where it gets kinky, now." Joe James was all ears again.

"She asks me to help pull her pants down and she takes forever again lowering herself onto the toilet. And all she does is let out this horrendous fart. Nothing else. Then she asks me to pull her pants back up and help her off of the toilet and back out into the Emergency Room. I get so grossed out and so pissed off at her, that I excuse myself and go outside. There, I take a piece of adhesive tape and cover up the name on my name pin. Then I take off my pantyhose and put one leg of them over my head you know, to distort my features, the way burglars do. And even though we don't wear caps anymore, in the fantasy, I take my cap and pin it on my head over the white stocking. Then I go back in the bathroom and beat her to a bloody pulp with her walker."

"That's sick" was Joseph James, III's official diagnosis.

17

"Wait, there's more" Dot said in a voice that reminded Courtney of her old friend Maggie Ruggles from Philadelphia. It was that same sick sense of humor. The same cynicism. Only somehow, it was easier to take coming from So What, Dot. Or maybe it was just because Courtney was fast becoming accustomed to the gallows humor of hospitals . . . and police work.

Dot was intent on finishing her story. "After I finish beating the crap out of her with her walker, I fill out an incident report stating that I found the patient in the bathroom, lying on the floor all bloodied and bruised. I check the box that says the patient was senile before the incident. Then I write in the extra space provided that 'patient **states**' "nurse beat me with my walker". What do you think? Huh, Doc?"

Joseph James, III turned to Courtney and said, "I think, that this innocent, young nurse here, should be kept away from you until she knows, like the rest of us, that you're only kidding." Then he signaled to the bartender to give Courtney a refill. "You'll need it" he warned.

"Funny" Courtney quipped. "Dot said the same thing about you."

That's when Mike Murphy interjected. "O.K. Doc, we're all been telling you about our dreams, what about yours? You get any weird ones? I mean, the kind you can talk about in front of the ladies here" he said gesturing to Courtney and Dot, as he signaled the bartender for another round for them all. Courtney didn't see how she was ever going to be able to keep up with these people.

"The only bad dream I have is after I do the yearly physicals on the police department" Joe James answered in what he thought was a clever tone.

"Police physicals?!" exclaimed Mike with exaggerated indignation. "Why I'm sure you've never seen such fine physical specimens as us" he said with great pride.

"Oh, it's not so much the physical exam I mind so much" grinned the good doctor. "It's just that every time I give one of you guys the rectal exam, I'm afraid one of you might ask me out."

That line broke the whole place up and even Joe was impressed with his own unexpected wit. "In fact, come to think of it," he continued, trying to get as much mileage out of the joke as he could, "I do sometimes have a recurrent nightmare. I dream that my rubber glove breaks." This was pretty good, especially for Joe James. He was obviously in rare form tonight. He usually was when he was showing off for a new "Babe" like Courtney Quinn.

"How about you, Courtney? Don't you ever have any strange dreams?" Joe asked. "I mean, everybody does. Why don't you tell me one and I'll see if I can interpret it for you."

The ice could beers on the sultry, muggy night must have gone to her head. Courtney was feeling good. And it felt so good to feel good. She wanted to be a part of the brotherhood in this place. She wanted to be a part of the party. And before she knew it, she heard herself say, "Well, yes. I do seem to have this crazy recurrent dream lately."

"Don't keep us in suspense." Dot said and Mike Murphy and Joseph James, III, and practically the whole rest of the bar, were all ears. Even Boris,

18

the Rotweiler partner of Stoner the Loner, perked up his second ear, though he was well past his third beer.

"Well, the dream usually has something to do with being naked in a public place" Courtney shyly began. You could hear only the effervescence of freshly poured drinks as she continued "Sometimes I'm in a shopping mall, or sometimes I'm just walking down the street. And once, I was even in **CHURCH.** All of a sudden, I notice that people are staring at me and I look down and realize that I'm stark naked. I wake up and I still think it really happened. I feel really embarrassed and uncomfortable for awhile." The bar was completely silent as most of the patrons tried to get a mental picture of this. Courtney knew the beers must have gone to her head, otherwise she would never have shared information like that with a bar full of strangers. Well they were mostly strangers.

Joseph James, III looked deeply into her eyes and said in the most convincing and professional tone he could muster, "I understand. I think dreams like that show that you have a deep seated need to expose yourself to someone. Someone you feel you can trust. Someone, perhaps, a lot like me."

Groans and guffaws filled the bar and everyone went back to their usual bantering and drinking and unwinding. Everyone that is, but a rather nice looking man, probably another cop, who sat across the bar from Courtney and made no inappropriate comments, even though she had left herself wide open for it. He seemed very gentlemanly as he sat there in his P.B.A. jacket, sipping his first and last beer of the night.

Courtney knew that she had had enough to drink and desperately wanted to go home. She was tired. And she was embarrassed. And she had to let Zachary out before going to bed. Poor Zachary. He was probably wondering where she was so late. She had never left him alone this long before. She gathered up her purse and said goodnight to everyone she had met at the bar. Joseph James, III tried to talk her into letting him give her a ride home in his red Corvette, but Courtney caught So What, Dot's warning glance, and graciously declined. Besides, she wasn't ready to have to fight off any persistent admirers. She still needed a lot of time to herself. A lot of time to do some much needed healing.

She slung her purse over her shoulder and headed for the door. She was a little nervous as she approached it, since a rather curious looking man sat there with a dog at his feet that looked half crocked. The dog, that is. Just as she was about to walk past them to the door, she felt a gentle tug on her arm. It was the man who had been sitting across the bar from her and wearing a P.B.A. jacket. An off-duty cop, she supposed.

"I heard what you said about your dreams over there" he said sincerely. "Don't listen to those guys. You're a big girl. You know what they want. They haven't got the first clue what a dream like that means."

"And you do?" She was flirting with him, but he was so cute.

"I believe so" he said, with incredible sincerity.

She stood there, touched by the kindness in his voice. Wanting only to listen to this kind and sincere man.

"I can see that you've been badly hurt. It's written all over your face." Courtney didn't know why, but tears sprung to her eyes. He noticed, but he continued, undaunted. "Dreams like that, naked dreams, usually mean you're feeling terribly vulnerable about something. As if you have nothing, no armor to protect you."

How could he possibly know this? She knew immediately down in her gut somewhere, that his interpretation of her dream was the correct one. She was overwhelmed that someone else could possibly know, possibly understand all the pain she was going through.

"My name's Father Murphy" he smiled kindly. My friends call me Padre. I'm the hospital chaplain and the police chaplain. If you ever want to talk about it, I have an office in your hospital down on the main floor." He covered her quivering hand with his. His offer was innocent and sincere and generous. "Don't hesitate to call if I can help" he smiled, just before she walked out into the muggy August night.

Chapter Five

Getting Tough

"You were quite a hit the other night at Nine-One-One" said Dorothy McFadden as she and Courtney made their way through the chow line in the hospital cafeteria.

"What do you mean?" Courtney asked sincerely as she eyed yesterday's leftover chicken and decided the grilled cheese sandwich might be a safer bet.

"I mean those guys were all over me after you left, wanting to know who you are and if you have a boyfriend or husband" Dot continued as she took her chances with the leftover chicken. "I haven't had that many guys pay attention to me since I hit a royal flush in the casino last year".

Courtney didn't know whether to take her seriously or not, but one thing was for certain. She certainly enjoyed Dot's company. She was seasoned, but not really hardened. She was a top notch nurse but she had a great sense of humor. Plus she was a hard worker and Courtney liked that. Best of all, Courtney liked that Dot never probed into her personal life or tried to get any information that wasn't freely offered.

"So, do you?" Dot was saying.

"Do I what?" Courtney realized that she had been lost in her thoughts for a moment. Something she did a lot, since losing Paul.

"Do you have a boyfriend or a husband?"

Courtney had to laugh in spite of herself. "You know, I was just thinking how much I like you because you never ask me any personal stuff like that, and then you had to go and blow it."

"Hey, I'm not the one who really wants to know. It's the guys down in Nine-One-One. They're not gonna leave me alone till I find out for them." Then she looked mischievously at Courtney. "Never mind. Maybe you'd better not tell me. It could be more fun this way" she smiled devilishly.

"Who, exactly wants to know?" Courtney asked cautiously.

"Everyone."

They were through the food line now and hesitated a moment as they scanned the busy cafeteria, looking for two seats together. No such luck. You'd think maybe the food was good or something, but the truth was that the cafeteria was entirely too small to accommodate the number of employees it took to run a hospital of this size. But as luck would have it, Dorothy McFadden's trained ear picked up the high pitched beep of several "code beepers" going off all at once.

It took Courtney an extra second or two to notice the sound too and she turned to Dot and asked, "What's that?"

"That means we're in luck" Dot answered. "It means there's a code going on somewhere and all these starving people will have to vacate their seats. Now all we have to hope for is that it isn't in the E.R.. Otherwise we lose too."

But it must have been their lucky day. The code team was being called to the Coronary Care Unit. In just a few minutes, Courtney and Dot would have their pick of virtually any seat they wanted.

Amid the mid-dinner chaos of the cafeteria, interns and residents grasped beepers in one hand and stethoscopes in the other, as they ran in the direction of the code. Respiratory therapists lost their places in line and some knocked over chairs as they sprang to their feet and headed for the code, some leaving their untouched dinners for the second time in the last hour. "If this keeps up" one therapist was heard to say as he headed for the staircase, "I'll never need to diet again!"

"Look, there's a seat by the window" Courtney pointed out. "Let's sit there."

Dot and Courtney carried their trays over and, since it was such a lovely Summer's evening, they each sat facing the window. It felt good to relax for a few moments and get a glimpse of the outside world.

"Well, to answer your question" Courtney began, mostly for the sake of conversation, "No, I'm not married and no, I don't have a boyfriend."

"You're not queer are you?" Dorothy asked in all sincerity, but before Courtney could get far enough past the shock of the question, Dorothy went on. "Well, I'm just trying to anticipate their next question. You gotta admit, it seems awfully strange that someone as pretty as you isn't all caught up with some guy, especially one of these doctor types. You know that's what the guys at Nine-One-One are gonna think."

"Well, why don't you tell them to find out for themselves, instead of going through you?" Courtney smiled. She really like Dot, but she still wasn't ready to get close enough to anyone to let them in on the real goings on of her life. It still hurt too much. The only one she ever talked to about Paul was Zachary. There was something about those big, sad Basset Hound eyes that Courtney found very comforting. And besides, she knew that Zachary missed Paul every bit as much as she did.

But all in all, Dot was turning into a good friend. And who knew? Maybe someday when Courtney was feeling surer of herself and possibly even able to talk about Paul without crying, she would tell Dot about him. But not yet. She just wanted to enjoy their budding friendship. Dot reminded Courtney of Maggie Ruggles in a lot of ways. She was such a rough and tumble sort of person, yet she had a heart of gold. And though she was every bit as streetwise as Maggie had been, maybe even more so, she still was not as cynical or burned out as Maggie had been.

Courtney smiled at Dot fondly. "You remind me a lot of a nurse I used to know" she said.

"Is that good or bad?" Dot asked.

"Mostly good. She was one of the best nurses I ever met. She taught me more about nursing and hospitals than I even realized at the time."

"So, what ever happened to her? You talk like she's dead or something."

"She is."

Dot looked up from her reheated chicken. "From what? I didn't know nurses died."

Killed herself" Courtney said flatly.

"Thanks a lot."

Just then a third dinner tray plopped down beside Courtney and a male voice asked, "Mind if I join you?"

It was Joseph James, III, D.O. and he had choosen the grilled cheese sandwich over the day old chicken too.

Dot pulled out a chair for him and said, "Not if you don't mind getting me some extra cream for my coffee first". Joseph James, III was only too happy to oblige. "Can I get anything for you, Courtney while I'm up there?" he asked solicitously.

"No thanks" she smiled as he gave her a quick wink and hurried back to the coffee counter.

"Check out his arms" Dot said to Courtney as soon as he was out of earshot.

"What about them?"

"Look closely. Did you ever see **anybody** with arms that could fill up the entire sleeve of an O.R. scrub shirt?" Dot said without the slightest hint of admiration in her voice.

"Maybe he works out" Courtney answered logically. But she had to admit that the closer she looked, the more impressed she was. She had never really thought about arms being muscular enough to fill up a sleeve like that, but come to think of it, it looked pretty nice.

"They say he brings his scrub suits home with him and his mother takes a few tucks in the inside seam of the sleeves so it'll look like that. Ever see anyone else with perfectly pressed O.R. greens?"

Courtney hadn't noticed it at first She had simply thought that Joseph James, III made a very neat and tidy appearance. But now that Dot mentioned it, Courtney couldn't help but notice the way his greens were neatly pressed and his muscular arms bulged unnaturally from the altered sleeves. She had to chuckle. "Must all be part of the red Corvette syndrome" she jested.

"You got it, Quinn. See, I knew you had potential. I don't know why, but from the first day I met you, I knew there was something about you" Dot confessed. "That you were smart and that you were a fast learner. And believe me, that's gonna come in handy around here."

Joseph James, III joined them again, interrupting the "girl talk" but not the mutually mocking glances they occasionally stole of his "fake muscular bulk".

He was good company though and they enjoyed his dinner conversation, even though all three of them knew it was all for Courtney's benefit.

Just as Courtney had taken a bite of her grilled cheese sandwiche, Dot looked out the window in time to see what looked like a body go flying by.

"Jesus Christ" she said almost matter-of-factly. At the same time, several gasps were heard throughout the cafeteria as horrified hospital personal turned their attention toward the windows.

Dot's first impression had been right. It was a body. A seventeen year old male who now lay splattered on the concrete in front of City Hospital. A pedestrian, a young girl, who had just happened to be passing by on the busy street as the body fell from the sky like a scud missile, let out a horrified scream and took off running. Meanwhile a crowd began to gather and Courtney thought she recognized two of the police officers who showed up. Mike Murphy and his rookie partner Fred Gantz. She recognized them from Nine-One-One and decided to concentrate on trying to remember their names instead of concentrating on the spattered brains that were discoloring the street.

When she looked over at Dot, she had already gone back to eating her reheated chicken. In fact, most everyone in the cafeteria had gone back to eating their meals before anything else could interrupt them. Courtney looked at her grilled cheese sandwich and just knew she wasn't that tough yet. She'd get something later at Nine-One-One.

The story quickly spread, even before the news team and television cameras got there, that it had been a seventeen year old boy who had jumped from the twelfth floor. He had been waiting to be admitted to the psychiatric floor for acute and endogenous depression. Naturally, all kinds of jokes started circulating about the inefficiency of the Admitting Office and about the boy's psychiatric diagnosis. But nobody meant any harm by it. Courtney knew that much by now. It was simply a way of coping with the everyday tragedies of working in a trauma center. The ordinary person on the street would have been revolted by the gallows humor of hospital people, and rightfully so. Probably the only other people in the world who would understand this kind of humor were cops. Thank God for places like Nine-One-One, where one could go after work and be completely understood.

Chapter Six

"Jody the O.D."

When Courtney and Dot returned to the Emergency Room from dinner, they saw a sight that made them never want to eat again. There was a thirthyish man who weighed at lease five hundred pounds, stripped to the waist and sitting on a stretcher.

"What have we got here?" Dot asked the nurse taking the man's blood pressure. A nurse who desperately wanted to go to dinner . . . at least she **had** wanted to go to dinner before seeing the sight of this massive human being whose arm was too big to take an accurate blood pressure reading even using the thigh cuff. The nurse no longer wanted to eat, but she would have loved to sit down for a few minutes and have a peaceful - sugar fee - cup of coffee.

"Well, well, well. If it isn't 'Jody the O.D.'" Dot said answering her own question. "What did you do this time? Shoot up or drink a keg of beer?" she said in her matter-of-fact voice.

"I think a little of both" said the nurse tending to him.

"I think it was **more** than a little anything" the cop with the dog, standing in the background said. He looked vaguely familiar. It was that cop who always sat by himself in Nine-One-One, unless of course, you counted his partner, Boris the Rottweiler who was attentively standing at his side at the moment. Courtney was trying to think of his name. Oh, yeah. "Stoner the Loner." She thought his first name was Frank, but she wasn't sure, so she just called him "Officer".

"Did you bring him in, Officer?" Courtney politely asked "Stoner the Loner". "I just need to know for our records" she added, trying to get through some of the paper work while So What, Dot took over the man's physical care, so the other poor exasperated nurse could sit down for a few minutes.

"Me and my partner here, Boris, brought him in" said Stone the Loner as Courtney began recording the information.

"You smell like an old urinal" said Dot to Jody the O.D. as she let the pressure out of the cuff around his arm, satisfied that the drug addicts and drunks rarely died in the E.R.. She had been a nurse long enough to know that they really only died on the streets, either in gunfights or knife fights.

"I smell because this Mother fucker made his dog piss on me when I was too weak to get up" he said pointing to the police officer and his dog. Dot suppressed a smile.

"Well, I had to see what kind of shape you were in. You looked unconscious to me" the officer said without the slightest hint of apology in his voice.

"I was in great shape" protested Jody the O.D.. "I was just a little high, that's all."

"Well if that's your idea of perfect shape," said Stoner the Loner, burying a firm finger into the fleshly pectorals of Jody, "then men better start wearing brassieres".

"You know, I'm getting sick and tired of the abuse I get in this place. You people are always picking on me. The service in this place **sucks**."

"If you know what's good for you, you'll shut up and let these nurses do their job. And while you're at it, you might want to thank your lucky stars and whoever it is that watches over scum bags like you, that these nurses are kind enough to take care of a slimeball like you."

"I don't have to take this" muttered Jody the O.D..

"Yes you do," countered Dot. "You've got a nasty cut over your eye that looks like it's gonna need some sutures" she continued as she cleansed the wounds that looked like they might have been inflicted by the butt of a flashlight. She'd seen enough of them to know what had gone on. And she knew enough to tell the patient if he hadn't been so high, he might remember how he'd "hurt himself".

"I gotta take a leak" said Jody the O.D., knowing full well that he could never win in this place. He was outnumbered. He knew how cops and nurses were. Always defending one another. Always taking care of one another. He'd like to see them try to function out there on the streets. It was a different world when you had no job, no home and worst of all, no fix. But that still didn't give the cocksucker cop the right to make his dog piss on him. And that reminded him again. "I gotta take a leak" he said, twice as loud this time.

"You know where the bathroom is" said Dot. "You've been here enough times before."

Jody the O.D. carefully lowered his massive and gelatinous body down off the gurney and headed for the Men's Room.

"He shouldn't be allowed in there" said Stoner watching him. "He's not a man, he's an animal."

Just then, a panic-stricken Joseph James, III came running up to Dot. "Dot, Dot!" he exclaimed, trying to control the terror in his voice. "We just got a call. They're bringing in a guy with an ax in his head!" Joseph James was terrified because he'd only been on call a few times so far in the E.R. and he'd never taken care of anyone with an ax in their head. But he knew that if anyone would know what to do, it was So What, Dot.

True to form, the first words out of Dot's mouth were, a loud, sarcastic and resounding, "**SO WHAT!**" Then she continued with, "This is an Emergency

Room, not a clinic". Joseph James, III or "J.J.", as she liked to call him, felt better already. Just the sound of Dot's competent, yet unperturbed voice comforted him.

"Quinn, you stay with Jody the O.D., get some silk sutures ready and I'll help J.J." she ordered, then took off in the direction of the crash cart, giving pointers to her enthralled audience of one as he grabbed a bottle of Maalox from his lab coat and took a big, white lipped swig.

Courtney's attention was drawn to the men's room as she thought she'd heard a lock turn and realized that Jody the O.D. had been in there an awfully long time. She looked up at Officer Stoner the Loner with a question in her eyes . . . and he had an answer for it.

"There's only one thing Jody's more afraid of than my partner Boris, here" he said. "Needles."

"Needles?" Courtney was incredulous. I thought he was a junkie?"

"He is" said Frank Stoner, "But a lot of those guys are like that. They don't mind if they're getting high from it, but the minute they think someone is going to prick their delicate skin with a needle for no good reason but to suture them up, they go a little haywire. We never should have let him go in there by himself. He's probably got himself locked in there by now. I've seen him do it before."

"So what do we do?" asked Courtney, not wanting to bother any of the overwhelmed medical personnel with a problem like this right now.

"Usually they have to call Hospital Security. Those guys usually try to talk him out of there, but they never succeed. Next, they try to get one of the doctors that he knows and trusts to talk to him, but that usually doesn't work either."

"So what do we do?" Courtney liked that Officer Stoner was generously sharing her problem as though it were just as much his.

Before he could answer, another police officer who had come in behind them with the man with the ax in his head, had a suggestion.

"I don't see what the big problem is" said Fred Gantz, partner of Mike Murphy, who was also standing there. Apparently both officers would rather flirt with a pretty nurse who has to find a way to get a fat man out of a locked bathroom, than watch a trauma team pull an ax out of some one's head.

"Well, we could always take the door off the hinges and drag him out of there" Mike Murphy said, sounding just as blasé as you would expect So What, Dot to sound.

"You're not listening to me" piped up Fred Gantz, better known as Howitzer Head Fred, since getting his new perm. "There's a much easier way, I'm telling you."

They all turned and looked at him mutely and expectantly.

"The guy weighs a good five or six hundred pounds, right?"

They all nodded. Howitzer Head Fred continued.

"All we have to do is get a pizza, tie a string to it and slide it under the door. Then when he goes to grab for it, we just keep yanking it till we pull it underneath the door again. Believe me, he'll go for it. My money says he'll be out of that bathroom as soon as the pizza man can get here to deliver it."

Even Mike Murphy had to laugh at that. "Yeah, but taking the door off the hinges can be done faster than 'Tony's' delivers." They all agreed and before she knew it, three police officers were taking the door off the hinges of the men's room. And they were right. It was done before the pizza arrived.

They forced the protesting Jody the O.D. back onto the gurney and Courtney went about setting up the equipment for the intern to suture up the nasty cut above his eye. When Jody saw the array of sutures and syringes of

Xylocaine, he began freaking out again. This time he had to be restrained. Firstly, because he was just a plain unreasonable person, and secondly, because his high was wearing off and he was in desperate need of another fix. It took all three police officers to hold him down while Courtney applied the leather restraints. Jody kicked and thrashed and even got a pretty good knee into Courtney's chest as the officers concentrated more on holding down the flabby, tree-like arms of the drug addict. Finally, when all restraints were applied and Jody knew he was beat, he took one last shot at his captors. He worked up a gob from the bottom of his lungs and spit it in their direction. Howitzer Head Fred was the unfortunate target, and Jody hit a bull's eye right on his cheek. Fred totally lost it at that point, but knew he couldn't very well beat up a restrained man . . . without it looking like police brutality. Instead, to everyone's surprise, he very calmly walked over to the secretary's desk, plucked a long, feather leaf from a plant there and stuck it up Jody the O.D.'s nose. The feather leaves no doubt tickled the drug addict's nose as he thrashed his head from side to side to avoid it. "What's the matter, Jody" said Fred with false sympathy. "Ya got a itchy nose?"

Jody muttered curse words under his breath, not daring to say anything aloud in this position.

"We'll see if we can get Miss Quinn here, to get you something for that. I think it comes in a nice, **BIG** needle."

With that Jody the O.D. quieted down and not another word was heard from him.

So What, Dot came over, looked at him in his four point leather restraints and said, "Nice work, Quinn".

"What happened to the guy with the ax in his head?" Courtney asked.

Mike Murphy laughed before Dot could answer. "He probably sevened out, right Dot?" he said.

Courtney was confused. "What does 'sevened out' mean?" she asked.

They all laughed. Even Stoner the Loner. Apparently she had missed something.

"You haven't been in Atlantic City very long, have you?" asked Frank Stoner, keeping a tight leash on Boris, who desperately wanted to harass Jody the O.D. some more.

"About a month" Courtney answered truthfully.

"Ever go to the casinos and play Craps?" asked Fred Gantz, somewhat sympathetic to what it was like to be the new kid on the block.

Then it made sense. Courtney didn't know much about playing craps, but she knew that when you sevened out, you lost your bet. Your game was over. That must be what they meant. The guy with the ax in his head must have "sevened out". He must have died.

"Yeah" said Dot, "We coded him and I even gotta say, J.J. did a pretty good job, all things considered. But there's no way that quy was gonna make it. He sevened out on the way to the O.R., poor slob."

Courtney looked at her watch. It was almost 12 midnight, a half an hour after their shift had officially ended. "Is that it for us, Dot?" she asked, anxious to sit down and have a bee.

"I think so" answered Dot. "The only other thing I know of that's going on is a "Code Brown" in cubicle 6."

"What's a Code Brown?" Courtney asked, not really wanting to know at this hour.

Dot laughed. "Just smell for it. It means someone has been incontinent of stool." She looked up at the police officers. "Sounds delightful, doesn't it fellas? Don't you wish you had gone into nursing instead of police work?"

All three police officers, four, if you counted Boris, turned to leave. "Will we see you two down at Nine-One-One later?" Fred Gantz called over his shoulder as they made their way out the door.

"You can count on it" Dot and Courtney answered in unison.

Chapter Seven

The Nightmare Begins

Patrolman Mike Murphy was a rare bird. No one could ever quite figure him out. First of all, the guy was really smart. He read every book he could get his hands on and he had a real ear for languages too. There was a story about him and his former partner, who retired last year (hence his new and much disliked partnership with Howitzer Head Fred, the rookie). Mike Murphy and his old partner, Greg Matthew's, had gone on a little vacation together in Aruba. Since the island is half French and half Dutch, Greg was afraid that the language barrier might be a bit of a problem, since all he spoke was english, with a "New Joisey" accent no less. But Mike Murphy had surprised everyone but himself, by his ability to pick up not only the basic language, but also the several different dialects he'd heard spoken. Greg was amazed. Mike was only too happy ordering his favorite drinks in the native tongue of the island, to give much thought to his talent for languages. After a few days he was able to speak enough of the local dialect to converse with taxi drivers and actually get them to where they wanted to go.

There was no doubt about it. Mike Murphy was a smart and talented guy. That's why no one could ever figure out why he never wanted to get promoted. Then again, maybe that's part of what made him so smart. He knew where he was happiest. On the streets and behind a bottle of Jack Daniels. Too bad his wife could never see it that way. But she couldn't. She'd said that being a cop's wife was stressful enough, without having to cope with the added burden of a husband who drinks too much. She loved her husband every bit as much as he still loved her, but she had to draw the line. And in weak and sentimental moments, Mike admitted that she probably was right. On top of the loneliness of missing his wife, he really missed his kids too.

It had been eight years since Dora had packed them up and left him. Their ages had been six, nine, eleven and fourteen. Now they were grown, or almost grown. Now they were fourteen, seventeen, nineteen and twenty-two. The oldest, his only daughter, was married now and expecting a child of her own. Mike had tried to remain close with his children, despite the separate living arrangements and he had to admit that Dora had been more than fair about visitation privileges and never speaking ill of him in front of the children. He was extremely appreciative of that, since he had heard so many horror stories from other cops whose kids grew up resenting them because of the angry and vile attitudes of ex-wives.

Mike Murphy was proud of his children, and his wife, for that matter. His family was the most important, in fact, maybe the only important thing to him. But Jack Daniels seemed to be equally important, much to his own dismay. Nonetheless, he was not only well-read and a bit of a polyglot, but he was every bit as streetwise as he was scholarly. He just didn't hide his street smarts as well as he did his intellect.

He was sitting on his usual barstool at Nine-One-One, trying to drown out the voice of his partner, Howitzer Head Fred, with one Jack Daniels after another. Mike Murphy wasn't a man who liked to show any emotion, good or bad. That had been part of the problem with his marriage, according to his ex-wife. He'd much rather drink Jack Daniels till any and all emotions faded away into some recesses of his alcohol-soaked brain. As he listened to Fred Gantz drone on about the suicide from the twelfth floor of the hospital tonight and the fat guy they should have tried to lure out of the bathroom with a pizza, Mike figured he could drink as much as he wanted, till Gantz's monotone was drowned out. Hanging around a half-medical place like this had taught him that human beings only used some ridiculously small fraction of their brain cells in an entire lifetime. He liked that thought, even if it was just a rationalization for everyone to drink more. He figured, with a brain like his, he had plenty more brain cells to spare, just waiting to be numbed by some Jack Daniels.

That's when So What, Dot and the new nurse, Courtney Quinn, came strolling in, looking like they could use a whole lot more than the usual "light beer" that they usually ordered.

"Rough night, huh ladies?" Mike Murphy called across the bar to them as he raised his glass.

They each smiled and nodded and took a long swallow of their beers simultaneously. And though they bore absolutely no physical resemblance to each other, they were beginning to behave like twins. It was a curious thing to Mike's observant mind.

They were followed shortly by Joseph James, III, better known as "J.J." since Dot had given him that nickname, solely because he hated it. Predictably, J.J. sat down next to the two women and ordered them all a round. He gulped his first one right down, then unhesitatingly ordered a second.

"Don't you think you better slow down a bit?" asked So What, Dot with more than a little concern in her voice. "After all, you **are** on call tonight."

J.J. just shook his head in a "no" answer as he slugged his second beer. "I got Reynolds to cover for me."

"C'mon, J.J., it couldn't have been all that bad" insisted Dot. "In fact, I think you handled that code with the guy with the ax in his head pretty well. It wasn't your fault that he sevened out." Dot didn't often give praise this freely, but she could tell that J.J. was extremely troubled tonight.

"Ah, c'mon" called Mike Murphy from across the bar. "Be a man about it. Whatever it was that freaked you out tonight, beer is for 'wusses'. Be a man and have a **real** drink" Mike suggested as he indicated to the bartender to give J.J. a Jack Daniels. On him.

31

"J.J., what's wrong? I've never seen you like this" Dot continued to probe.

"Well, right after you guys left, some taxi cab driver brought in some young girl. He found her out on the street. She was all beat up and raped. The guy apparently slashed her throat and left her for dead in an alley, but the girl was ballsey enough to drag herself out onto the sidewalk where a cab driver was passing by and picked her up."

"Well, well, well." said Mike Murphy. "Will wonders never cease? You mean there's still actually a good Samaritan left in Atlantic City?" He was on his third Jack Daniels and he was getting ugly. "Besides, how do you know it wasn't the cab driver that raped her and beat her and then made himself look innocent by bringing her to the hospital?"

"There were witnesses" answered J.J. as he stuck to his beer, knowing he would regret drinking anything stronger. "In fact, there was a married couple in the cab at the time. They're the ones who spotted her lying on the sidewalk and told the driver to pull over."

Fred Gantz had been listening, intrigued. "Is she gonna make it?" he asked.

"Doesn't look good" said J.J. feeling like a failure.

"Any ideas on who did it?" he asked with rookie enthusiasm.

"Hard to say" answered J.J.. "He cut her up pretty bad and slashed her throat. All she could do was gurgle. We couldn't get much information out of her before she went to the OR."

"Did she have anything else besides the slashed throat and the rape?" asked Dot, all nurse for the moment.

"God yes" answered J.J. "It was horrible."

This got everyone's attention. He looked around at his captive audience and went on. It wasn't often you could shock and hold the attention of a group like this, but stories about pretty young girls who got slashed up always hit a nerve, so to speak.

"Well, when we put her up on the table to examine her, we noticed a shiny little sliver of metal alongside of her nose. We had no idea what it was, so we got a stat skull x-ray. Turns out, the dog who did this to her, must have stabbed her in the face with a knife, then broke the handle off. The blade went completely through her skull. She must have fought like crazy, because the tips of three of her fingers on the left hand were cut off. She must have put her hand up to protect her face and the guy sliced her fingertips off before getting the knife into her face."

J.J. was visibly shaken, but the hard core audience wanted more. "We had to trach her right there in the ER. Obviously she couldn't do any talking, so we just had to examine her from head to toe for injuries. She probably has plenty more than what we saw, but we had to get her to the OR right away for the life threatening ones."

"How old was she?" asked a captivated Fred Gantz.

"Not sure" answered J.J., beginning to sound more like a detective now than a doctor. "She didn't have any I.D. on her. That slime bag probably took her purse, too, with all her identification. She looked to be about twenty or twenty-two. Somewhere in there, I'd say. But it's pretty hard to tell with the face slashed up and the swelling."

"So the family, if there is one, doesn't even know yet, I guess, huh?" asked Fred sadly.

"Who're they gonna notify" Mike asked sarcastically through his Jack Daniels haze, successfully making Fred Gantz feel foolish for asking such a "rookie-ish" question.

"All I know" continued J.J., "is that she must have been a pretty girl. She had long dark hair with one of them, what do you call it? French braids? And she was tall. She had pretty green eyes too. That's an unusual combination. You know, dark hair and skin with light green eyes."

Mike Murphy didn't know if it was all the drinking or what J.J. had just described, but suddenly he felt like he was going to topple off the barstool. The girl he was describing sounded an awful lot like his daughter, Devon. Hah, it couldn't be. She was probably safe and sound right now at home with her dentist husband. Besides, she was four months pregnant with their first child. She was probably in bed with her feet up at this very moment. Just the same, Mike Murphy had a very uneasy feeling about his daughter. Call it an instinct. Call it over protectiveness. Call it anything you want. But Mike Murphy knew he had to get to the phone and make a very important call. He expertly slid off his barstool, never giving the slightest hint that his stomach felt like there was a bar room brawl going on inside of there. He took his drink with him, purely out of habit and began making his way toward the phone in the vestibule. He would have used the one behind the bar, but he didn't want anyone to hear him being an over anxious father.

Just as he rounded the corner of the bar, he heard J.J. add something that made the glass in his hand take on a life of it's own and jump out of his hand, crashing to the floor.

"Oh yeah. The worst part was that she's pregnant. Looks like about four months along, I'd say."

Mike dialed his daughter's number with fingers that trembled so badly that finally he had to get the operator to dial it for him. There was no answer. Well maybe that wasn't so bad. Where was Dennis, her husband? Maybe they were out together somewhere. Yeah. That must be it. They must have gone out on the town, especially since they knew their nights of this kind of freedom were numbered. Only about five more months of freedom left. Mike felt a little better. He ambled back inside to his seat as her heard Stoner the Loner state matter-of-factly, "must of been a Brother."

"Yeah" agreed Dot, sipping sadly now at her beer.

Courtney was curious abut the logic behind the assumption, that the assailant had been Black. "Why do you say that?" she asked, knowing she was about to learn another "Atlantic City Lesson".

"She came in from a mostly Black and Puerto Rican section of town" answered J.J. "Not many white people in that section of town."

"So how can you be certain it wasn't a Puerto Rican?" she persisted.

"I'll handle this, fellas" Dot said, as she drained her beer and signaled for another one. "You can tell by the stab wounds. Hers were deep and straight in. that's the way your friendly neighborhood, 'Black Boys' do it. Puerto Ricans do lots of superficial slashing. You get to know the difference once you work around here long enough."

"No other clues?" Gantz asked J.J. again. "I mean nothing that would tell you anything about who she is or who did this to her?"

"Not really. And we're not even sure she's gonna live long enough to tell us what happened or to give us any kind of a description. She's a fighter apparently, but she's in pretty tough shape right now."

Mike Murphy was getting uneasy again. He didn't like this. There was too much coincidence here. His beautiful daughter was tall and dark and had the kind of light green eyes that everyone remarked on. And she was four months pregnant. He wasn't about to sit here any longer. Maybe Devon **was** out with her husband. Or more likely yet, maybe they were in bed and had turned the phone off. Well, let them all think he was an over protective father. Maybe he was. But he was also going down to City Hospital right now to find out who the hell this poor girl was. Or wasn't.

The pallor of Mike Murphy's face as he put his empty glass down on the bar and headed for the door, escaped no one. Father Murphy, who had been sitting on the other side of Mike and silently taking it all in, said nothing. He simply rose and put an arm around Mike Murphy's surprisingly solid shoulders, as both men unobtrusively let themselves out into the steamy, moonless, August night.

J.J. looked at Fred Gantz for a clue. "You don't think . . ." But he never finished his sentence. Everyone was thinking the same thing.

Chapter Eight

Shock and Trauma

"There's a good chance it's not her, Mike" Father Murphy said as he got in on the passenger side of Mike Murphy's Toyota Corolla. "There are an awful lot of twenty-two year old girls with dark hair and green eyes in this world."

Mike said nothing. He just stared straight ahead as he darted through red lights and stop signs on his way to City Hospital. The laws meant nothing to him at this point. The Padre's reassuring words meant nothing to him at this point. In fact, nothing meant anything to him at this point . . . and nothing ever would again.

"I want to see the girl they brought in about an hour ago who was beaten and raped" he demanded of a familiar looking night shift nurse in the Emergency Room.

"She's still in surgery" said the nurse with cool efficiency.

Father Murphy knew there would be big trouble if he didn't intervene before Mike let the Jack Daniels do his talking for him. "Excuse me, Nurse" said the Padre, "We heard the girl had no identification on her and my friend here thinks he knows who she is. We're afraid it might be his daughter" he added, almost inaudibly.

The nurse looked at Father Murphy's collar, then at the buldge of Mike's off duty revolver and uttered, "Wait here. I'll be back in a flash." And she was. She made a quick phone call, then summoned an orderly to escort the priest and the police officer up to the operating suite where the patient would be coming out of surgery momentarily.

It was the longest walk of Mike Murphy's life. Everything was in slow motion, including his own speech. It was like what they called "out of body experiences." He felt as though he were outside of himself, watching his Jack Daniels infiltrated body walk in slow motion behind the orderly and beside the Padre. The other men stepped back and allowed Mike to enter the elevator first. He guessed they were being polite to the father of the dead girl. He supposed they were each wondering who was going to break the news to him. But they needn't have worried, he already knew. He wasn't sure exactly **how** he knew, but he figured it had something to do with this curious "out of body" feeling he was experiencing.

The victim was still in the Operating Room, but the surgeon had sent word that Mike and the Padre could change to OR greens, scrub up and come in to see if they could identify the girl, even though she was still under anesthesia. Her potential for life was that precarious. They would rather have her identified while she was still alive. And nobody really wanted to guess how long that would be.

Mike Murphy and Father Murphy entered the operating room together, just as a technician was asking a saddened "What about the baby?" question. The doctor answered tersely before realizing they had company in the room, that the woman was not going to make it and that the fetus was entirely too premature to even consider any kind of extraordinary measures. Though Mike had never once in his twenty-two year career been hit by a bullet, he knew what it was like now. The doctor's words hit him like several dozen bullets, all at once and Mike reeled unsteadily on his feet from the blow.

The doctor looked up just as Father Murphy helped Mike to steady himself. "Hi ya, Mike" said the doctor, recognizing him from years in the Emergency Room. "You want to step up here a little closer and take a better look?" He asked with nothing but kindness in his voice.

The nurse stepped aside and the cop and the priest stepped into her place. Mike Murphy recognized the face of his beautiful daughter instantly. It would be hard to explain to any one else, but there is no scar so deep, no swelling so severe and no wound so brutal, that a father wouldn't immediately recognize his own child. A jury of his peers might question it, but a parent never would.

"It's Devon" he said hoarsely. He felt the touch of Father Murphy's hand on his shoulder that was meant to comfort. But there would be no comfort. Not ever again. Only revenge. Besides wanting his daughter to live, revenge was what Michael Murphy wanted most in his world.

Devon Murphy-Donahue made it out of the OR and into the Recovery Room. She wasn't doing well, but the nurses and doctors seemed surprised that she had even made it that far. Mike Murphy stood beside her, holding what were once the beautiful, tapered fingers of his beloved and semi-conscious daughter, while detectives tried desperately to question her as she drifted in and out of consciousness. Father Murphy knew Mike's time with his daughter was very limited and very precious, so he left him there as he went to perform the task of notifying the girl's husband and mother. It was a task he would never want to have to live through again.

Mike studied Devon's edematous, bandaged left hand with the three fingertips missing, yet still with the gold wedding band on. Apparently, the finger had been too swollen to remove the gold band before surgery. He studied the sutures in her lovely face, where the knife had entered and been broken off. And as grotesque as she may have looked to an outsider with these brutal injuries, she was still the most lovely and beautiful woman he would ever know. She was his daughter, his baby, and **nothing** anyone could ever do, could make her less than beautiful to him.

The detectives were trying to get a description of the beggar who had done this to her. A crime, especially a crime like this, against a brother officer or his family, was like a crime against the entire Atlantic City police force. They would find this slime ball, no matter how long it took. And they would make him pay. They were all, each and every detective at her beside, yearning for even the slightest clue that she could give them. And yet, the best they could hope for was a nod or shake of the head to the yea or no questions they could ask, since Devon could not verbalize anything with an endotracheal tube in her throat, hooked up to a ventilator. Oddly enough, it was her distraught husband, Dennis, who provided them with the only clue that night. And even **it** wasn't much to go on.

Dennis Donahue, DDS, had arrived within ten minutes of receiving the phone call from Father Murphy. He said his wife had gone out shopping earlier in the evening around six to get some earlier forgotten groceries. Dennis had offered to go, but Devon had insisted that she'd like to stop off and visit with her girlfriend, Diane, on the way home. Dennis then decided he would go to a Board Meeting at the hospital for the Department of Dentistry since Devon wouldn't be home till later anyway. They would have a late dinner, after each had arrived home. When Devon hadn't arrived home by 9 PM, Dennis had called Diane. Diane said that Devon had never showed up and she had just assumed that perhaps she had been feeling too tired to stop over. Dennis then went out looking for her and that must have been where he was when Mike had tried to call him earlier. He eventually contacted the police station and had sat there for some time, filling out forms and leaving his phone number with them. In all his agitation, he'd forgotten to mention that Devon's father was a cop. Maybe it was because Dennis never saw very much of Mike or maybe it was because he was so distraught that he never thought to mention it. Not that it would have changed the outcome, really. Dennis just may have been notified of the tragedy sooner, that's all.

Anyway, the taxi driver had picked her up at about nine-thirty. God only knew exactly what time the attack had occurred and how long she had lain in the alley that she was finally able to crawl out of.

Devon Murphy-Donahue finally gave in to death in the arms of her husband and with her father still holding onto his daughter's beautiful, bandaged hands. The detectives were understanding and sympathetic, but they wanted to talk to Dennis to see if he could give them anything, **anything** to go on.

And he did. Sort of. For some reason, known only to a person in mourning, Dennis noticed what turned out to be a significant detail. He noticed that Devon was missing the earring that she always wore on her left ear. He noticed because they had gone through a sort of "hippie" stage when she had convinced Dennis to wear an earring. She said it mad him look like a "Bad Boy" and she liked that look, especially because he was really such a "good, conservative boy". Dennis had agreed to do it for her and they had bought a pair of earrings in New York one night, after dinner and a show. One of the earrings was a little gold half moon, which Devon wore in her left ear with a little diamond stud in the right ear. The other half of the pair was a little gold circle with a star on it, and Devon had insisted that Dennis wear that one in **his** left ear. They had done that some two years ago and promised to always wear them. And they always had. Until tonight, that was. Dennis noticed that

Devon's little gold half moon earring was missing, yet the diamond stud was still in the other ear. If the guy had stolen the earring to hock it, why hadn't he taken the diamond stud too?

Mike Murphy was too numb to think about stolen earrings at this point and didn't think it was much of a clue. In fact, he had often wondered about the mentality of his son-in-law, or any guy, for that matter, who went around with an earring in one ear - dentist or no dentist.

Suddenly Mike wanted desperately to get out of that hospital. He didn't want to answer any more questions and he didn't want to have to deal with the grief of his ex-wife or his son-in-law or the pain and agony of his other children. He was too engrossed in his own pain. And he needed a drink.

Word had already spread to Nine-One-One when Mike Murphy and Father Murphy arrived, looking like they had just fought a war. Bars in Atlantic City had the luxury of not having to close at all. They only closed when they wanted to clean up, and in Nine-One-One, that was a rare occasion. The two men had secretly hoped that everyone would be gone by this hour. It had to be after three o'clock in the morning, and neither man wanted to echo the morbid occurrences of the evening. No one asked them to. Most everyone had stayed and waited quietly. No one had anything much to say to Mike, because that was the way they knew he wanted it. They just sat there, letting him know in their own wordless way that they were his friends, and that they were there for him.

Courtney and Dot were among the group that wordlessly waited for the two world-weary men to return to the tavern. Like a couple of homing pigeons, everyone knew that sooner of later, they were bound to show up. Mike Murphy was despondent and it showed. Father Murphy appeared doleful and a bit withdrawn, yet he couldn't help noticing, once he settled down on the barstool next to Mike, that Courtney Quinn looked a bit peculiar. It was nothing he could put his finger on, not like she'd had too much to drink or anything like that. There was just suddenly a side to her he'd never seen before. She was only drinking club soda at this point, but there was definitely something peculiar about her expression when the two men came through the door.

After Mike and the Padre had lifelessly put down their first round of drinks, Father noticed Courtney leave a few bucks on the bar and gather up her purse as if to leave. She said a quiet good night to the people near her, but instead of heading for the door, she headed toward Mike Murphy and the Padre.

She put a gentle hand on the unaffected shoulder of Mike Murphy and simply whispered, "I'm sorry". Mike didn't have any intention of acknowledging her. The only person he had any interest in was Jack Daniels. He liked old Jack because he didn't talk back and because there was never a need to say anything to him, especially in moments like this when there was absolutely nothing to say.

Father Murphy caught Courtney's elbow as she turned to leave. "He can't help it, Courtney" he said kindly. "He's been through a lot tonight. He's in shock." He hated to see a sweet girl like Courtney get her feelings hurt. But he

38

had no idea that she understood even better than he did, what Mike Murphy was going through right now.

"It's OK" Courtney smiled at the Padre. "I understand a little bit about what he's going through."

Suddenly Mike Murphy burst back to life again - an incredibly angry surge of life. "What could you possibly know about this kind of thing!" he shouted, lifting his muscular and bulky frame from the barstool and suddenly towering over her. Everyone else jumped up to subdue the distraught man, but they really didn't have to. Courtney didn't flinch. She really **did** know how this man felt right now and she got some of that old despondent feeling back herself. Tears sprang to her eyes and no one had to touch Mike Murphy as he listened to a twenty-six year old woman who obviously had had her share of incredible pain too.

"I know it feels like something dead is living inside of you," she said. "Even though no one in the world can possibly know what kind of sense that makes. It feels the way those pregnant women must feel, who are told that their fetus is dead, but that they'll have to carry it to term anyway. You walk around knowing that you're carrying something dead inside you. You're like a body carrying around a dead soul. You feel like you're already dead inside, but it just takes the outside longer to die."

God, this girl really did know what it was like. Mike Murphy sat back down and sipped at the fresh glass of Jack Daniels the bartender had put before him. Father Murphy and the rest of the group stared at Courtney through new eyes. They had all known there must have been something she hadn't been telling them, but no one ever guessed that someone so young had been hurt so badly.

Courtney wasn't finished. She stood there boring holes almost right through Mike with pale blue eyes that were filled to the brim with tears and Mike found himself wondering why the tears didn't spill over. Like Courtney on the day of her husband's funeral, he found his mind being distracted by all kinds of bizarre thoughts.

"And it gets worse" he heard her saying. "Eventually you feel like you're sitting on the bottom of a hole that's so incredibly deep, you can't even see the light at the top. You stop believing that there **is** any light. And I wish I could tell you that there is, but I just don't know yet myself."

There it was. The tears finally could contain themselves no longer and erupted from her pale blue eyes. She didn't even notice. She was intent on what she was saying. "You see Michael Murphy, I had a husband once. He was a cop in Philadelphia. He was the best. The best husband and the best cop you'd ever want to meet. But he got killed because of some senseless thing like this, like what happened to your daughter. And I blamed everyone out there for what happened and sometimes I still do."

Father Murphy, among others, was in complete and utter shock at this point. They had all thought they'd had all the surprises they were going to get for one night, but Courtney Quinn had given them all a sucker punch. It came out of nowhere and unexpectedly. And God, they were all so sorry.

"And one more thing," Courtney was speaking directly to Mike. "You're gonna hear a lot of pretty words from people in the weeks and months to come, things like 'God's will' and "Tincture of Time' and not one of those words will make you feel any better. The only people comforted are the people who are saying it. But don't blame them. Don't blame us. People just want to help you, and no one knows how. You and I don't even know how. I won't even try, cause I know it won't do any good. I just want you to know that you're not alone. And that, even though it could never, in any way help your pain, I **do** know what you're going through."

That said, Courtney unselfconsciously slung her purse over her shoulder and headed for the door. All eyes followed her and everyone was left dumbfounded and speechless. Most of the group ordered a night cap at that point. It was going to be a sleepless night for a lot of people.

But Courtney Quinn would go home, take the dog out, and go right to bed. And for the first time, she would make Zachary sleep on his little pillow on the floor instead of in the bed with her, as he had become accustomed to doing. Not only that, but for the first time since she had lost her beloved Paul, she would sleep like a baby. The healing process had begun.

Chapter Nine

Typical Traumas

September is hurricane season. And a pretty rough hurricane was predicted to slam into Atlantic City any time after seven o'clock this evening. Both the police department and the City Hospital Emergency Room would be hopping if the weathermen were right. And they were.

At first, it was just a heavy rain and the police officers dealt with all the usual motor vehicle accidents that are usually caused by slick streets and reduced visibility. They sent quite a few "accident victims" over to the Emergency Room. Some had actual injuries that could use a suture or two, but most were just the usual, "Wait till I call my lawyer, I have severe whiplash" type injuries.

As the evening wore on, the storm worsened. The winds were so severe out of the southeast, that the rain began to look as if it were coming down horizontally. It was a night fit for neither man nor beast, Frank Stoner thought as he and Boris drove around in the patrol car marked "K-9 Unit". That label usually served him well and at the very least, got respectful, if not intimidated looks, especially from out of towners. But tonight, Frank could do without the special courtesies some of the drivers occasionally showed him, as he drove with Boris's big head panting in the passenger seat window. Frank and Boris would rather be anywhere than driving around the streets on a night like this. And even though it was only late September, there was a definite hint of crisp, Autumn nights in the air. At least they <u>would</u> be crisp, as soon as this rain let up. Frank and Boris both were wishing they could spend the entire night at Nine-One-One. If Boris could count, then they **both** would have been counting the hours till they got off duty and could unwind with a couple of brewskies tonight at their favorite watering hole.

Just then Frank Stoner noticed what looked like a body lying in the gutter. He figured it was probably a drunk or a drug addict. In fact, it looked a lot like Jody the O.D., who was hard to miss since he weighed more than the sewer pipe he was trying to crawl inside of at an abandoned construction site. Frank honestly didn't care if Jody the O.D. got hit by a skidding car or, less likely, washed down the sewer, which in Frank's opinion, was where he belonged. But it was bad public relations for people to see some "poor homeless guy" drowning in a hurricane as a police officer drove by and ignored him. Frank knew he had to stop and pick him up and **do** something with him, just so all the local "do gooders" would be happy. He wished he could let boris get out and piss on him again, but obviously it wouldn't make much of an impact in this storm.

41

Frank pulled the patrol car over and got out, covered from head to foot in his bright yellow rain gear. At first he called Jody by name, then, convinced that there were no witnesses, he used the heel of his boot to kick him onto this back so that he could positively I.D. him. It was Jody all right. And he was higher than the Big Dipper - and in about as much of a cloud right now. He must have been in another street fight with another one of his drug addict buddies, because there was blood oozing from somewhere on his massive body. Frank didn't really want to find out where the blood was coming from. He really didn't care. And he wasn't about to touch this dirtball. God only knew what kind of disease he could pick up. Especially since AIDS was such a well known possibility these days.

He ordered Boris to harass Jody and force him into as much of an upright position as possible. Then Frank ordered Jody into the back of the police car, with Boris right beside him, panting his dog breath into Jody's face. Frank knew that technically he could have called the First Aid guys, but, hell, he was already here, and he hated to make anyone come out on a night like this if they really didn't have to. Besides, it was only Jody the O.D.. There'd be no problem or no great loss if he sevened out in the back of the patrol car.

Frank thought about the poor nurses in the ER who were going to have to examine and treat this slime ball. At least he had been able to get him into the patrol car without actually having to **touch** him. But those poor nurses were going to have to touch him. He hated to do this to them. He really had to give those nurses and doctors credit sometimes. He didn't know how they did it. But as long as they had to do it, he hoped that cute little Courtney Quinn was on duty tonight. Dot too. They made a great team and Courtney was pretty easy on the eyes. He was still in shock though, that she had been married to a Philadelphia cop who'd been killed. If it hadn't been for the night she had spilled her guts out on the bar, the night Mike Murphy's daughter had been murdered, no one ever would have known. She had made it a well kept secret. She was quite a person. The kind of woman a guy could really respect. "Oh, shut up" he suddenly told himself. "There you go getting all sentimental about a woman you hardly even know. Cut the shit." But he liked Courtney Quinn in spite of himself. And in spite of the fact that he knew she would probably never go for a guy like him. He wasn't exactly Mr. Personality and she probably had plenty of offers from all those doctors she worked with. But deep inside, he knew he shouldn't even be thinking this stuff. He wasn't good at relationships.

Some ER attendants helped him haul Jody the O.D. onto a gurney and lug his massive and rain-soaked body inside. The ER looked pretty busy and Jody would have the good fortune of having to wait for his rather minor wounds to be tended. The way things looked, that meant he might be able to wait out this entire storm in the dry, warm ER, instead of outside in a sewer pipe that he really couldn't fit into.

Frank looked around and spotted his two favorite nurses on duty, Courtney and Dot, but they each looked awfully busy. Courtney was wearing some kind of get up that Frank had never seen before. She was covered from neck to ankles with a long sleeved, yellow isolation gown. That wasn't too unusual, but she also had some kind of a scrub cap covering all of her hair and leaving only her pretty and delicate face exposed.

"Hi, Frank" Courtney smiled as she continued donning her protective gear. Now she was putting on a surgical mask and after that, pulled down a pair of clear plastic goggles over her lovely blue eyes. She was donning a double pair of rubber gloves when Frank asked, "Are you about to perform surgery or are you one of those people who have to live in a plastic bubble?"

Courtney laughed. At least, he thought she did, even though he couldn't see her friendly smile behind the disposable mask. "I have to give a blood transfusion" she explained.

"You have to put on that get-up every time you transfuse a patient?" asked an amazed Frank Stoner.

"It's called universal precautions" she answered matter of factly. "I have to start this I.V. and give him two units of packed cells. I'll probably be in there for quite a while."

"Aren't you afraid of getting AIDS or God knows what?"

"Not as long as I take the proper precautions" she said like a true professional.

"I couldn't do it" declared Frank.

"I know" Courtney answered, leaving Frank to wonder just how she meant that since he couldn't see a facial expression to give him a clue, before she turned and brought the bag of blood in with her.

Frank then turned his attention to So What, Dot who was busy working with J.J. and an Orthopedic resident, on a patient who apparently had a broken neck. They had the patient lying on something called a Stryker Frame. It was a narrow, stretcher type of bed on which a patient could be sandwiched between two board-like pieces and flipped over onto either their back or their belly, without disturbing the crucial placement of traction. One slip of the traction that stabilized the fractured vertebrae in the neck and the spinal cord would be cut and then it would be "Quad City", complete paralysis from the neck down. Frank liked hanging around the Emergency Room. There was always so much to learn. It was a fascinating place. But right now everyone seemed pretty busy and Jody the O.D. started acting up and yelling that he wanted some "service" around here. He was the least sick and had the biggest mouth. Typical.

Finally, J.J. who found it impossible to concentrate on his patient with the broken neck because of all the noise that Jody was making, calmly approached the drug addict with one hand behind his back. J.J.'s lips were covered with a thin, white layer of Maalox, as usual, but he looked completely in control. He spoke calmly to the irate and somewhat frenzied Jody, who was coming down off his high and letting everyone know it. Suddenly and competently, J.J. exposed the syringe that had been behind his back and plunged it into the beefy arm of Jody the O.D.. No one cared enough to ask what was in the syringe, but Jody quieted down remarkably within minutes.

43

"J.J., get over here, quick!" yelled Dot from the Stryker Frame patient. "We're in trouble. I can't get a blood pressure!"

J.J.'s whole face turned as white as his lips.

"Better bring the crash cart!" Dot yelled.

People, lots of them, technicians, nurses, orderlies and J.J., crowded around the Stryker Frame. J.J. knew he was the doctor and that they were waiting for some kind of direction from him, but he honestly didn't know where to begin. He often cracked under pressure in situations like these. And Goddammit, where was that Orthopedic resident who had been here a few minutes ago? Technically, it was Ortho's patient.

"She's got a weak pulse, but I'm still not getting a blood pressure on her" reported Dot.

"Open up the I.V.'s. Let the fluids pour in" demanded J.J., finally sounding like a doctor.

"I already did" asserted Dot.

"Shit, let's get her in Trendelenberg" J.J. commanded as he began to move the levers on the frame that allowed him to put the patient in a position with her feet up and head down, known as the Trendelenberg position. Just as he moved the final lever and was about to put the patient's head down as far as it would go, the frame seemed to be jammed. It wouldn't budge. Then he realized it was because Dot's strong and experienced arm was deliberately preventing it.

"You don't want to do that" she said in a low and confidential voice.

"Why not?" asked J.J., totally bewildered. Everyone knew that when someone had a dropping or absent blood pressure, the first thing you do is position them with their feet above the heart.

"She's got a broken neck" Dot reminded him. "If you put her head down, you'll lose the traction and the alignment of the fracture and then she'll be a Quad."

J.J. was terrified. "What should we do?" he asked honestly.

"Start another I.V. in the other arm and pour more fluid into her" was Dot's expert answer.

It worked. Little by little the patient's blood pressure became palpable, then audible through the stethoscope. Dot heaved a sigh of relief and J.J. left to calm his frazzled nerves for a moment. The patient opened her eyes groggily and slowly looked around. "What happened?" she asked, becoming more and more alert.

"You gave us a little scare. Decided to lose consciousness for a minute" Dot said, sounding completely unruffled. "You're O.K. now" she added reassuringly, wondering if the patient would ever have any idea how close she had just come to being a quadriplegic.

The patient looked up at Dot. Then she noticed J.J. returning (probably from the men's room), and with adoring eyes she said, "Isn't my doctor wonderful?"

44

No one ever heard Dot's reply because just at that moment a scream was heard from cubicle 6, the cubicle where Courtney was transfusing her heroin addict patient with the low hemoglobin. Courtney emerged looking as though she had just been shot. There was blood spattered everywhere.

"It's OK" Courtney assured her co-workers who raced to her aid. "I'm all right. He just scared me, that's all."

It turned out that the patient Courtney had been transfusing was a very angry and resentful drug addict who also had a drinking problem. He'd been diagnosed with a bleeding ulcer a little over a year ago and was a pretty steady customer in the ER ever since. He frequently came in when his red blood cell count was low, received a transfusion of packed red blood cells, a prescription for Tagament and was sent home. Courtney had felt sorry for him tonight as she had put on all her gear before going in to start his I.V. and transfuse him. She got to thinking how isolated he must feel and how, at least in the hospital setting, he rarely got to see anyone's whole face, without it being shielded with masks and goggles. She knew the patient had a reputation for being ornery, but she foolishly thought that perhaps a little compassion on her part might go a long way. After she'd got the transfusion started and had monitored the patient's vital signs carefully for the first hour, she decided to let the patient feel more like a human being and less like a Leper. She decided to remove her gloves and goggles and mask and at least let the patient see another human face. She didn't feel she was risking anything, since she wouldn't have to have physical contact with him again until the transfusion was completed. She decided to stay in the cubicle while she did the paperwork involved and try to have a civil conversation with him. That's when, out of the corner of her eye, she saw a bag of blood with the plastic catheter on the end, that had formerly been in the patient's vein, come flying through the air at her. It caught her across the legs as she screamed and tried to jump out of the way.

Frank Stoner was almost as angry with Courtney as he was with the patient. How could she have been so foolish? So trusting? Didn't she believe yet that it's a jungle out there? That you can't trust **anyone**? That most people don't know how to appreciate compassion? Though life had already taught her some pretty harsh lessons, Courtney Quinn apparently still had a lot to learn.

Frank watched her as she stripped off her remaining gear and headed for the utility room to wash up. She passed J.J. on the way. Frank could tell J.J. had the hots for her, but with his Maalox covered lips, he didn't stand the proverbial snowball's chance in hell. It completely negated the imaged he tried so hard to portray with the red Corvette and the custom tailored scrub suits. If only he'd quit drinking that shit, or at least wipe the traces of it off his mouth, he might not need the fast cars and semi-bulging muscles to impress the women. But Frank certainly was not going to be the one to tell him. Especially where Courtney Quinn was concerned. No sir, it was every man for himself.

Courtney smiled up at J.J. and Frank got a little nervous until he heard her say, "J.J., you look a little pale tonight. Especially around the lips."

"I need a nurse" J.J. said in what he thought was an enticing tone.

"I think what you need is a couple of units of packed cells" Courtney laughed as she walked off toward the big sink in the utility room. Frank was relieved. Courtney was no fool after all. One of these days, when he got his nerve up, he'd ask her for a date.

Frank turned and went back toward the patient he'd brought in, Jody the O.D.. As he approached the cubicle where he'd left him completely plastered from whatever was in that shot that J.J. had given him, he had to laugh out loud. There was Dot standing over the snoring fat man, plastering a sign over the bed with hospital, non-allergic tape. The sign read:

YOUR TAX DOLLARS AT WORK

Chapter 10

High Tide

The wind was whipping the rain into little needles that stabbed at your face and any other uncovered portions of your body as the "regulars" literally blew in the door of Nine-One-One. And it wasn't even the height of the hurricane yet.

Stone the Loner was sitting at his usual table away from everyone else at the bar, with Boris at his feet. They were both on their second beer when Dot and Courtney hung onto the big brass handle of the door as they "blew in" off the rain-laden street. They settled down on the vacant barstools next to Mike Murphy with the ever-present Father Murphy at his side.

No one was really surprised that Mike hadn't taken any time off after the funeral of his daughter. He couldn't bear the incredible sadness of sitting home with the rest of his bereaved family and talking morbidly of old times. He didn't see how anyone could do that. Nah, give him a rundown, dilapidated section of town to patrol and a few Jack Daniels afterward and he'd be about as happy as possible for a man who had just been through the most devastating experience a human being could endure. His biggest advantage in coping with the overwhelming grief, was that he didn't wait for it to get better. He knew it never would. He just spent his days working the busiest districts he could get himself assigned to, working overtime, and spending most of that money on Jack Daniels at Nine-One-One. The only perceptible changes to the others was that he didn't seem to hate his rookie partner, Fred Gantz, anymore. It wasn't that Howitzer Head Fred had done anything to win Mike's loyalty or respect. It's just that Mike didn't care anymore. He didn't care enough to love and he didn't care enough to hate. In fact, he didn't care enough in any way to even care. The only thing he ever thought about besides where his next Jack Daniels was coming from was revenge. He would find that guy some day . . . and he would torture him. The way he had tortured Mike's Beautiful daughter and her family.

Father Murphy always stayed close to Mike, especially when he was drinking, which of course, was most of the time. The Padre didn't exactly trust the vacant stare and outwardly calm appearance of a man he knew was boiling with rage on the inside. But so far, Mike had been robot-like and very closed-mouthed about any plans for revenge.

It had been a little over a month now, and there was not the slightest clue of who had done this heinous thing to Devon Murphy-Donahue. And being the experienced police officer that he was, Mike Murphy knew that the longer it went on without a resolution, the less chance there was of ever finding the guy. But who knew? He would keep his eyes and ears open. Oftentimes, crimes like this were solved by a serendipitous traffic ticket or some completely chance encounter like that, instead of the months and sometimes years of carefully detailed police work. Besides, there were a few clues to go on.

The night the ghastly incident had occurred, Dot remembered something that would possibly help. She and J.J. had treated and released a man for minor cuts and bruises, most of them to his face. The man said his name was Sam Steward and that he was thirty years old, but he had no identification on him. He claimed to have just had a fight with his girlfriend, but one look at this wounds told them either his girlfriend was a Sumo wrestler . . . or a terrified and tortured girl who was fighting for her life. The man had had several long scratches down his face that looked like they had been inflicted by fingernails. Dot remembered that he also had an odd looking tattoo in the little web of the left hand between the thumb and the forefinger. She had noticed it for two reasons. First, the colors were still vivid as though he'd had it done recently. Second, it was a tattoo of a big long rattle snake with an evil expression on its face and wearing a top hat. And about the only thing Dot hated in this world more than drug addicts, was snakes.

The patient had brought himself in for a few sutures in the face and a few steri-strips on the more superficial scratches on his arms. He had called no family and had been released without giving any significant information about himself, which was not an unusual occurrence on a busy night in a busy ER, like that of City Hospital. The patient had come in a few hours before the taxi driver had dragged in the barely alive body of Devon Murphy-Donahue, and Dot just couldn't shake the feeling that they had actually treated the animal who had done this to her. It was just a feeling. But it was a strong one, and Dot trusted it. So did Mike. The detectives weren't quite as impressed. No matter. As far as Mike Murphy was concerned, he would be on the lookout for the rest of his life for a thirty year old Caucasian male with a tattoo of a Rattle Snake on the web between the thumb and forefinger of his left hand.

Dot settled on the barstool next to Father Murphy and Courtney took the one next to her. J.J. was the next customer to "blow" in the door, and naturally, he gladly took the empty seat next to Courtney. He had just ordered his on call club soda, when his beeper went off. Usually he liked it when that happened in front of pretty women, so they could be impressed that he was a doctor. But Courtney already knew that and he would rather stay here and flirt with her than have to go make a phone call. But duty called and Joseph James, III trudged off to see what it was. His mother would have been proud.

No sooner had he vacated his stool next to Courtney, than a semi-miracle seemed to have occurred. Stoner the Loner pulled Boris up on his leash and joined real people at the bar. Of course, Stoner took the stool next to Courtney (even though J.J.'s club soda was still there, marking his place) and then he coaxed Boris to jump up on the empty barstool next to him. Courtney (and everyone else, for that matter) was astounded, both at Stoner's sudden social graces and at Boris's agility in getting on and balancing himself on a barstool.

49

Especially after two beers. Stoner ordered Boris another round, just for being such a good little show off.

"Frank, that's great" laughed Courtney. "How did you ever train him to do that?"

"Survival" answered Frank as he nodded toward the floor.

So that was it. Frank wasn't being suddenly sociable and Boris wasn't training for the circus. The tide was coming in and the raging hurricane was, inch by inch, inundating the floor. Frank didn't particularly want to get his feet any wetter than they already were and he certainly didn't want Boris to catch a cold by lying on that wet floor. Wisely, Frank and his partner moved to higher ground.

J.J. was too busy looking down at his water logged feet, to notice that Stoner had taken his very prime seat. "Hey Stoner" J.J. said, after getting over the initial shock of seeing Frank at the bar, among people. "You're in my seat."

"Not any more" Frank answered as Boris stared warningly at J.J.. Frank continued in a knowing voice. "You just got a call. I heard your beeper go off. You know it's a guarantee it'll be something you'll have to go in for instead of handling it over the phone" he said expertly.

"How do you know that?" asked J.J., actually quite impressed.

"Because it's a stormy, lousy night and stuff like that always happens on these kinds of nights. There is no justice, J.J." Frank smirked as he took a gulp of beer

"I don't really have to go in" J.J. said defensively. "It's just some old lady with chest pain. I can have the nurse run an EKG on her and call me with the results."

Dot put down her beer loudly for emphasis. "Haven't I taught you **anything**?" she demanded loudly of J.J..

"What's the big deal?" J.J. answered defensively again. "It's just some old lady with chest pain. It's probably gas", he said, trying to add humor, but nobody laughed.

"Listen, J.J. and listen good" began Dot. "How many times do I have to tell you? Chest Pain to a doctor is like a gas leak to the gas company. Any time somebody even **thinks** they smell gas, whether it's on a holiday or the middle of the night or what, the guys in the gas company are obligated to put on their hard hats and go out and check it out. Chest pain's the same way. There's always that one in a million chance for a disaster. Now go put on your hard had and go check it out."

J.J. disgustedly, but obediently, began to put the raincoat back on that he had just peeled off and headed for the door.

"I'll have a beer for you," offered Stoner the Loner. Then he turned to Courtney, looked down at the inch of water that was surrounding the bar and rising fast and said, "Well, I guess you're stuck with me. At least till the tide goes out."

Chapter Eleven

Low Tide

Father Murphy stuck close to his spiritually wounded friend, Mike Murphy. Not that he had any choice tonight. They would all be pretty much stuck where they were till the damn tide went out. Until then, it would be impossible to abdicate their barstools without immersing their feet in the salty and nippy waters of the brooding Atlantic Ocean.

The good Padre was very concerned these days about the reticence of his usually gregarious and sarcastic friend, Mike Murphy. The lack of sarcasm and cynicism was the worst part. Father Murphy was not only used to Mike making some pretty crude and disparaging remarks, he sometimes actually looked forward to them, in spite of himself. Mike Murphy, though very caustic at times, had a way with words and could be very funny. He could unintentionally bring much needed humor, and as a result, perspective, into an otherwise discouraging and cruel world.

But Mike Murphy had lost all sense of perspective lately. And probably, Father guessed, his sense of humor was gone forever. Not that anyone could blame him.

"Mike, what do you say I ask Sam for a key to a room and you spend the night here?" Father asked protectively, noticing that, as usual, his friend had had way too much to drink. It had been happening often and Room #10 upstairs in Nine-One-One was beginning to become Mike Murphy's home. Not that anyone minded or didn't understand, least of all the owner, Sam Manetti. Sam was no stranger to tragedy himself. He had lost a child many years ago in a drunk driving accident, which was when he started the rule about anyone who'd had too much to drink, especially the hospital people and cops, were always welcome, if not encouraged, to sleep it off upstairs . . . free of charge. Sam knew exactly what Mike was going through, and worse yet, what he would continue to go through, and he was happy to support him in any way. Like everyone else in Nine-One-One, Sam and father Murphy both understood Mike's aversion to going "home" alone and to spending any time by himself, thinking of his terrible loss. By the same token, both men also knew that the day would come when Mike would **have** to face the dreadful misfortune that had changed his life forever. Both men also knew that these things take time. And that each individual has his own little time clock already set inside him that would tell him when he was ready to start facing the harsh reality without hiding himself behind compulsive over-working and/or Jack Daniels.

"Didn't you tell me you have court in the morning?" asked Father Murphy, subtly suggesting that Mike consider sleeping it off now so that he'd be ready to testify in court in the morning about a case involving a major robbery from one of the casinos.

"So what," slurred Mike, sounding a bit like "So What, Dot". "I don't give a shit what happens."

Father Murphy knew Mike didn't really care about anything any more, but he knew he had to at least put on the appearance of caring if he wanted to keep his job. And he **knew** he wanted to keep his job. For all his complaining, it was the only thing that stood between Mike Murphy and the complete loss of sanity.

"Mike" said Father Murphy gently, "I thought you told me you had to go to Grand Jury in the morning."

"More like 'Grand Story'" answered Mike with a pronounced slur in his words this time. "All I gotta do is go in there and exaggerate enough so that those slimeball lawyers will have no choice but to prosecute and lock up those scum buckets that ripped off the casino. No problem. I could do it in my sleep" he added, as he put his head down on the bar and allowed an almost frightening snore to reverberate from his palate, before his head even made it all the way down to his waiting arms on the bar.

Sam Manetti gave the Padre a knowing look. He understood all too well what hell on earth was, and that Mike Murphy had been the quest to most recently check in. The Padre extended his hand and Sam Manetti dropped the key to the usual room #10 in it. Fred Gantz half-heartedly slid off his barstool into the now three inches of ocean water surrounding the bar and grabbed Mike Murphy under the arm on one side. Father Murphy did the same thing on the other side and together they semi-dragged, semi-walked Mike up the stairs to his waiting bed. Mike was getting used to waking fully clothed these days. It saved him the trouble of getting dressed for court in the morning.

So What, Dot had a lot of trouble seeing Mike Murphy in this much pain. Mike and Dot had worked a long time together, all things considered. Mike bringing the sleezeballs into the Emergency Room for some twenty-two years now and Dot taking care of them for the last eighteen. And even though there were plenty of people out there who weren't sure that she still had an ounce of sensitivity left in her Emergency Room, tragedy-weary bones, it cut Dot to the core to see Mike suffering like this. She didn't want to watch any more and she didn't want to hear the concerned and morbid conversations that would take place about him as soon as he was safely tucked in bed. She wanted to leave before any of that started. She gathered up her purse and said goodnight to Courtney and Frank Stoner, who was still trying to put the moves on her. Poor Courtney. Dot could only assume that when J.J. came back from checking out the "gas leak", the lady with chest pain in the ER, he too, would be back to flirt with Courtney and try his best shot. But Dot couldn't be responsible for Courtney's social woes. Courtney was a big girl. Dot was sure she could handle herself. She picked up her purse and waded through the rising tide within the bar. The hurricane must be really kicking up out there.

"How do you stand your job?" Stoner the Loner was saying to Courtney as Boris indifferently lapped at his third beer. "I mean, the usual stuff we bring in to you guys is bad enough, but don't you get tired of helping people who don't even appreciate what you're doing?

"As a matter of fact, I do" Courtney answered, feeling the beer go to her head. "But it's not always like that. Besides, it's my job. I'm sure you don't like every aspect of your job, right?"

"You got that right" answered Frank Stoner, "But at least I got a gun and I can shoot them if they start giving me any shit."

"That would only cause more work in my job" Courtney laughed.

"I'm glad you can laugh about it" said Stoner, "I think I'd refuse to do it. I don't care what kind of precautions you say you use, I still say you're risking **your** life every time you touch those people."

"Look who's talking" Courtney countered. "You wouldn't find me sneaking down darkened allies, bullet-proof vest or not."

Stoner thought he heard a hint of admiration in her voice and he liked it.

"Besides" she added, "what other jobs offer as much excitement and opportunities to do good as ours do? Think about it Stoner. We'd be bored to death doing anything else." Her voice softened then and she east her eyes downward. "Call me an idealist" she said, "but if it weren't for cops and nurses, I think the world would be a pretty ugly place."

There were a lot of thing Stoner could call a person like Courtney and "idealist" was only one of them. "Survivor" was another.

"I'd call you a survivor" Stoner finally replied. "Especially the way you're survived losing your husband."

Courtney didn't miss the sudden tender tone in Stoner's voice, but she still couldn't handle sympathy, no matter how sincere it was. She couldn't trust herself not to cry at the mere mention of Paul's name. Some survivor.

"Great veins!" she suddenly exclaimed pulling one of Frank's hands over to her and palpating one of the big, blue rubbery veins of his muscular hands. It was a great way to change the subject, she thought.

"They are?" asked Frank, fishing for a compliment.

"I'll say. I could get an eighteen in you easily!" She seemed really excited over his veins.

"What's an eighteen?" He was almost afraid to ask.

"Oh, it's a rather large sized catheter that we use to transfuse blood or any thick solution through. These babies would be a breeze: she said continuing to examine the healthy and abounding veins of Frank's left hand.

"Well, thank you, I guess" Frank said beginning to admire his lovely veins with their young, healthy blood supply coarsing through them. He could kind of see why she had taken a shine to such a manly looking hand.

He was just about to order them each another beer when he noticed that the guy across the bar was beginning to look a little strange. The man was not a regular, just some old guy who had probably just come in to get out of the storm. Frank wouldn't have noticed except that Father Murphy and Fred Gantz had just come down the stairs from dragging Mike into a room, removing his gun and propping him on his side in the bed . . . in case he decided to puke after all the Jack Daniels tonight. The Padre and Howitzer Head Fred, had just sat down at the bar and ordered a cold one, when this strange man seemed to waver, then lean into the Padre. Before anyone knew what was happening, the man slumped forward onto the bar. Everyone's first guess was that the guy was just drunk, but as the color drained from his face and he seemed to have stopped breathing, the place went into panic.

Howitzer Head Fred was the first to jump up and pull the guy's head up in case he was just drunk. Father Murphy, getting used to tending to the sick, felt for a pulse, in the big carotid artery of the man's neck. Howitzer Head Fred, noting the man's intense pallor, shouted (to no one in particular) "If he's pale, lift his tail! If he's red, lift his head!"

All action stopped momentarily, as the Nine-One-One crowd stared blankly at Fred.

"What?" said Father Murphy.

"It's an old boyscout saying. Helps me remember every time, what to do in a situation like this. If he's pale . . . " Nut he never got to finish.

"We heard you the first time" the Padre interrupted, a little impatiently. "Help me get him down on the floor. I can't feel a pulse. I think we're gonna have to do CPR."

For the second time that night, Father Murphy and Fred Gantz got their shoes soaked and played nursemaid to an unconscious drunk. In the meantime, Courtney jumped up and grabbed J.J., who was just coming through the door again after checking out the lady in the Emergency Room with the chest pain.

"C'mon" demand" Courtney as she grabbed J.J.'s arm. "We need your help."

J.J. would have followed Courtney **anywhere**, at any time. He was that attracted to her. But if he had known she was bringing him over to do CPR on an old drunk lying on the ocean soaked floor, he might have had second thoughts. Thoughts like, let the cops do it. They're trained in CPR. "I just want to sit for awhile and no one is letting me do that tonight. Could people please just quit dying till I have a break? Is that asking too much?"

But it was Courtney who was pulling him in the direction of the man on the floor and he couldn't resist following her anywhere. Even doing CPR with her didn't seem like such a bad way to start a relationship with her.

Father Murphy and Fred Gantz were only too happy to move out of the way and let the medical experts take over. Courtney automatically positioned herself to do the chest compressions. That's the first crucial lesson anyone who works in a hospital learns. It's the cleaner job. Less chance of getting puked on. Less chance of getting God knows what kinds of diseases.

J.J. felt for the pulse that he knew wouldn't be there. This just wasn't his night. He tilted the man's head back, pinched off the nostrils and placed a 4X4 gauze pad that he kept in his pocket for just such occasions, over the rubbery, slimy mouth of the victim. He looked at Courtney and said "O.K., let's do it."

Courtney began the chest compression's while her own heart was beating wildly in her chest. She began to count out loud, "One, one thousand, Two, one thousand . . . " Oh, God, she hoped someone had called the paramedics. The frantic and silent thoughts of both J.J. and Courtney were punctuated by the sound of aged and osteoporotic ribs crunching beneath Courtney's strategically placed hands with each compression. They exchanged horrified glances with each of the first few crunches of ribs, but they continued their perfectly synchronized CPR.

At long last, all kinds of people, with all kinds of equipment began to arrive. Big, masculine hands appeared beside Courtney's delicate ones and a husky male voice counted compressions with her. "One, one thousand, Two, one thousand, Three, one thousand, Switch-on-next-count."

Much to Frank Stoner's disappointment, Courtney was able to get up off her water-drenched knees. Frank had enjoyed standing behind her as she forced the lifeless man's heart to pump. He had liked watching her firm, young hips moving to the rhythm of the life-saving compressions she was delivering.

At the same time that Courtney had been relieved of her share of the CPR, an ambu bag came from somewhere and one of the paramedics relieved the grateful J.J. of having to do any more mouth-to-mouth resuscitation.

Courtney and J.J. each wanted desperately to get to a sink . . . for very good reasons. J.J. wanted to wash his mouth out with antiseptic and Courtney wanted to wash the feel of broken ribs from her hands. They could hear the paramedics shouting that they needed to cardiovert or "jump start" the heart with an electrical current, and since the patient and all of the paramedics were lying in or standing in a virtual swamp, since the tide had reached its height, it would be impossible to cardiovert until they had transported the patient and themselves to dry ground and dry clothes.

The man was loaded into the ambulance while the paramedics tirelessly continued CPR. It was finally over. What a night. Drinks were on the house at this point. And everyone needed one.

Courtney climbed up onto the closest stool, which happened to be the one between Father Murphy and Fred Gantz. Father Murphy smiled and raised his glass to her. "To Courtney Quinn" he said. "I think you brought us good luck."

"What?" she said, not believing her ears. "How can you say that? We've had nothing but bad luck, since I walked in tonight."

Father Murphy's grin only widened as he looked down at the receding water on the floor. "The tide is finally going out" he said.

55

Chapter Twelve

The Fantasy

"If I ever fall in love again, it will be with a man who loves music and all the old romantic songs like I do. He'll sing to me and he won't be shy about it. He'll like to dance too, but he won't be a show-off. He won't necessarily have to be a **good** dancer, just someone who is so attuned to my sense of rhythm and movement, that he anticipates my need for each move. Then he eases me through it and holds me when the movement demands a little physical support from him. And he makes me feel like a ballerina.

He'll think my sense of humor is one in a million. And when we're at a party, he'll plead with me to tell a particularly funny story again, even it he's heard it a million times before. And he'll think it's funny, each time I tell it. He'll beam at me with eyes full of laughter and let it be known that he is proud to be my husband.

He'll love me for all the things I'm unhappy about with myself. He'll think my cooking is fine, even though I know it could be a lot better. And he'll love me for trying so hard to improve on it. So I'll try even harder. He'll find it amusing that I sometimes get crazy about my weight when I think I'm fat. But he'd much rather I get a little carried away on diets sometimes, instead of getting carried away in the opposite direction. He'll support my striving for perfection, but he'll love me all the same, with all my imperfections.

He'll drive any kind of a car but a Corvette. He'll know what I think of guys who drive Corvettes and it will endear me to him. He'll own a motorcycle, but won't automatically assume that he's always the driver. He won't be afraid to sit behind me and let **me** be the one to decide where we're going. He'll trust that I can guide us on the bike just fine and he'll sit back and put his big, strong arms around my waist and murmur sweet nothings in my ear, over the roar of the engine.

He'll like money and the toys that money can buy for us, but he could never love money or toys more than he loves me.

As for making love, well, let's just say he'll do that the same way he dances."

Courtney looked down at Zachary's big Bassett Hound eyes that were watching her so intently.

"O.K., I'll stop now, she smiled at the dog. "I know I'm probably boring you to death. Besides," she added a bit forlornly, "the man I just described sounds exactly like Paul. I was lucky enough to find him once in a lifetime. I guess I have no business hoping for a second chance at being that happy."

56

Courtney bent down and put her arms around Zachary. He had patiently listened to this little daydream, time and again. He was a tireless and respectful audience. He never tried to gently remind her that there was no use in daydreaming, like people did. He never tried to tell her that her marriage to Paul was like a dance that now must remain unfinished. That she should put it behind her like everything else that was beyond her control. He never let on that he'd heard her tell this version of her dream man, his former master, a thousand times before. He didn't tell her that he ached for Paul too, probably as much as she did sometimes. No, good old Zach just sat there on the floor or the bed, staring up at her as though he were hanging on her every word, as though he'd never heard these stories before.

That was why Zachary was the only one she ever told her secrets to. He wasn't like people. He would never tell her to stop dwelling on the past and to get on with her life. He would keep it to himself when he would see her cry sometimes when something unexpectedly reminded her of Paul. He pretended not to notice or think it strange that she kissed her pillow goodnight sometimes when she couldn't stop aching for Paul with his big strong arms around her. Oh yes, the craziness had set in almost a year ago on that gruesome day when she got the phone call that the biggest and best part of her life was now over. Sometimes there were days when she thought perhaps she could see the end of the "crazies", but then, she would have other days when an end to the pain and insanity was nowhere in sight.

The one year anniversary of Paul's death would be coming up in just a few short days. Sometimes she wondered how she had made it through such a long, lonely time without him. Other times, she marveled that it had been a whole year, instead of just yesterday. No matter how long or short the time had seemed though, she knew she would dread the anniversary of a date she'd rather forget. She would have to go out and do something to help herself forget, though she had no ideas what.

And no matter how stalwart an appearance she put on in front of others, Zachary was probably the only one who ever had or ever would witness her true feelings, her tears and her timorous moments. No one else would ever guess. And Zachary would never tell.

"Imaginations are wonderful things, aren't they Zach?" Courtney said to Zach's reflection in the mirror as she brushed her hair. "In the imagination, anything is possible. Even bringing Paul Back to dance with me or talk with me or love me again, even just for a few minutes." She turned around then and smiled down at the dog before donning what served as a nurses uniform these days; white jeans, a blue (or any color, for that matter) Izod La Coste shirt, woolen socks and high topped sneakers. Caps of course, had been obsolete for years now, they just got in the way. Besides, nurses felt they contributed to the handmaiden attitude. And the sneakers or running shoes were the best part. She guessed no one in the "old days" of white dresses and white caps and rubber soled "Clinic" shoes ever appreciated that a nurse needs clothes she can

work in. She stared at her reflection in the mirror and figured Florence Nightingale was probably turning over in her grave now.

She filled her pockets with the equipment she would undoubtedly be using tonight; bandage scissors, hemostats (better known as clamps), non-allergic tape and a pink stethoscope. Then she pulled on her winter coat. It was early December now and the days were getting bitter cold. "Want to go out Zach?" she asked in anticipation of her possibly long absence, if she decided to stop at Nine-One-One after work tonight. Zachary must have been thinking the same thing. He jumped up and got his leash and brought it to her.

"You are a wonderful friend, Zach" she smiled, as she put the leash on his abundant neck. "Sometimes I forget you're a dog." Then she added, "But don't worry. I'll remember. Especially when it's time to come home and let you go out for the night."

Chapter Thirteen

The Lawsuit

City Hospital didn't know it at the start of the 3 to 11 shift that early December day, but they were about to become involved in the least defensible lawsuit their hospital lawyers had ever seen. There would be no defending what happened.

The shift started off routinely enough. It was bitter cold outside and the first snow of the season had fallen. That always meant an influx of chest pain and heart attack patients. These patients were usually old, out of shape men, whose macho pride or whatever you wanted to call it, kept them from paying a young, durable kid a few bucks to shovel their sidewalks and driveways. These patients were usually accompanied by worried, "I told you so" type wives, who looked even more terrified than their struggling spouses.

It was also close enough to Christmas that the party season had begun and the usual array of alcohol-induced injuries awaited treatment, but usually not anesthesia, in the cubicles that lined one side of the Emergency Room. Most of them were quietly sleeping it off while the medical personnel tended to the more urgent chest pain and heart attack patients.

And, naturally, in what should have been named after him, Jody the O.D. was sitting in his usual corner of the Emergency Room, coming down off a high and bleeding from what looked like knife inflicted wounds. Wounds that he had probably, once again, sustained in a fight over drugs with some of his "drug buddies". There was little doubt that Jody the O.D. would be dead last on the priority list. Tis the season.

There was one old lady with what looked like a fractured hip, but no one could get near enough to her to be certain. Every time anyone, doctor, nurse, or technician, came near her, she let out a scream and threatened to sue if they touched her. At first the staff tried to be understanding and patient with her. After all, fractured hips are very painful maladies. She had fallen in the revolving door of a local department store and had apparently screamed bloody murder when the paramedics and the police had helped move her out of the doorway. When they loaded her onto the stretcher and into the ambulance, they said they had never heard anyone curse like that. the cops and paramedics were impressed.

Meanwhile, here she sat, asking for help, but refusing to be examined or x-rayed. She was eighty-two years old and looked a little on the frail and arthritic side. The plan was to sedate her heavily and then try to examined and x-ray her. But apparently, she was as resistant to narcotics as she was to being examined. Seventy-five milligrams of Demerol didn't even touch her. She continued lying there, cursing up a storm when anyone came near her and complaining bitterly about the "service" around here. The staff just kept monitoring her vital signs as they kept pumping her full of enough drugs that would have kept Jody the O.D. happy for a week. Time was on their side. They knew her body would succumb eventually.

"You know there are two schools of thought on fractured hips, don't ya?" noted So What, Dot as she and Courtney exited the cubicle after giving the woman her third injection of Demerol. Dot was constantly teaching Courtney things she'd never heard of and Courtney was extremely grateful to be so chummy with this wonderful combination of nurse and teacher.

"No, tell me about it" Courtney answered, always eager to learn.

"Well, some people look at an old arthritic lady like that and figure that the hip fracture occurred when she fell in the revolving door because probably her hip took most of the impact."

"I can't image what else you could possibly think" Courtney said, fascinated that there would be any other explanation.

"Not so fast" said Dot. "Some people say, that the hip may be so arthritic and osteoporotic, that the it actually fractures first, then causes her to fall. It's the old question of which came first, the chicken or the egg? Well, in this case, the question is, which came first, the fracture or the fall?"

Once again, Courtney was amazed at Dot's vast knowledge of all different diagnoses. She hoped that someday she would know even half of what Dot knew. Honestly. She would be happy to know just **half**.

"We still better keep an eye on her. She's had an awful lot of Demerol so far, and she could easily just bottom out on us." Dot said with genuine concern in her voice. "Let's check her every chance we get. That kinda stuff scares me."

At that moment, Jody the O.D.'s voice could be heard above all the other chaos going on. "This place **SUCKS**! I'm never coming here again. This is worse than prison food!"

Jody the O.D. had been given a tray of food by one of the orderlies, hoping that stuffing his mouth full of food would be one way to keep him quiet. It might have worked too, except for when a big, well-fed looking cockroach came crawling out of his mashed potatoes.

Joseph James, III , D.O. came running up to Dot and in his best "doctor" voice, said loudly, "Dot, did you hear that? That's deplorable. A patient getting a meal tray with a cockroach crawling out of it! I want something done about it!"

Dot was completely unruffled. She looked J.J. up and down, not at all surprised that someone with his mentality would make a big deal out of a cockroach, while there were people with impending heart attacks in at least three of the cubicles.

"First of all, J.J." she started, deliberately using his nickname because she knew how much it humiliated him, "It's not a **real** patient. It's only Jody the O.D.. And, secondly, don't come around here with your silly, little problems. I got more important things to do than to tell you how to handle a simple situation like this."

J.J. looked apologetically at Dot. It wasn't because he was necessarily sorry, it was mostly because he knew he needed her. And the last person in the world he could afford to alienate was So What, Dot. He looked humbly at the floor, then brought his eyes back up to meet hers. "What should I do?" he asked in a subdued voice.

"Tell him it's an excellent source of protein" she said as she turned on her heel, leaving J.J. to wonder whether or not she was serious.

"C'mon Quinn, let's go grab a quick bite to eat. I'll tell the others. They can hold the lady for a few minutes. In the meantime, you go check on the swearing old fart with the hip. That Demerol stuff really bothers me."

Dot and Courtney left quickly so they could get to the cafeteria before it closed. They'd been so busy, they'd forgotten the time. Dot punched the elevator buttons impatiently, as if it would make the old antique elevators come any faster. "C'mon, c'mon," she grumbled. under her breath. "I swear these things never work" she grumbled. "You'd think in a hospital this size, they'd at least have elevators that work. They either don't come at all or they stop between floors and you have to jump down onto the floor. I'd like to have the money they spend fixing them. Fixing them and then they don't work."

"Well, at least it was the elevator that was responsible for putting a patient's dislocated hip back into place when she was on her way to the OR. Remember that?" Courtney laughed, trying to minimize Dot's frustration.
Just then the elevator arrived, but when the doors slid open, the car was a good foot above the floor. Dot and Courtney had to hold onto the doors and pull themselves up onto the elevator. "They can transplant human hearts" Dot mumbled, 'but they can't get an elevator to stop evenly with the floor."

They got to the cafeteria just as the workers were putting everything away. Forget the hot entrees, they had to beg to even get a cup of coffee and some left over chocolate pudding.

They were back in the bustling E.R. within minutes. They would have been back sooner, except for the lethargy of the hospital elevators. Courtney ran in to check on the old lady with the fractured hip and all the Demerol. It looked like the Demerol had finally snowed her and J.J. was in there applying a few pounds of Bucks Traction to the foot of the affected leg. Bucks Traction is a simple foam rubber boot with velcro straps that is attached to five or ten pounds of weight, depending on how much the patient weighs. It doesn't really do anything in terms of aligning the fracture. It's more of a reminder to the patient to hold still or that hip is going to **hurt**. The real reduction of the fracture and fixation of the bone is done in the operating room under general anesthesia. Since it's not considered an emergent procedure, it's not usually done' until the patient has had a full medical work-up, including blood work, urinalysis, a chest x-ray and an EKG. But if you ever saw the intensity on J.J.'s face as he applied the foam rubber boot that even an orderly could correctly apply, you'd think he was performing major surgery.

He looked up when he saw Courtney walk in and was glad to be seen doing such a "Doctorly" thing in front of her.

"She finally calmed down, huh?" Courtney said quietly, so as not to start another tirade of curses in case the woman was not completely sedated.

Yeah. We're gonna send her up to the floor now." J.J. said decisively. "We still didn't get an x-ray of the hip, even though a blind man could see that it's clearly broken. X-ray's been too busy with all the other stuff goin' on down here to waste their time fighting with this one. We'll just send her upstairs and get the x-ray done later, after she's properly sedated." Courtney was impressed. J.J. apparently had gotten hold of himself and was acting with some logic and decisiveness. Dot was teaching him well. Courtney went outside and called the orderly to transport the patient to the eighth floor, Orthopedics. Then she called the floor herself and gave the nurse a report on what had gone on down here and what to watch for, regarding the impressive amount of Demerol the patient had had.

It seemed like things were finally getting organized. Two of the three chest pain patients had already been transferred to the Coronary Care Unit and the third one's "chest pain" was beginning to look more and more like indigestion. It looked like he might hang around for awhile, and if all the blood work and other tests came back normal, he might have a pretty good shot at going home.

Yes, everything had calmed down, that is, until Jody the O.D. began acting up again. Apparently someone was suturing up one of the superficial stab wounds on his forearm and he was crying like a baby that just got its first immunization shot.

By this time Dot had had it with his antics and asked the intern who was suturing him, for permission to give Jody what was known as a "Molotov Cocktail", a mixture of Demerol and Vistaril in a syringe, and a Valium by mouth. That usually did the trick and should knock him out, at least until the forearm was adequately sutured.

The Molotov Cocktail did a stupendous job. Within minutes, Jody the O.D. was sleeping soundly and probably would have let them suture his mouth, if they had been so inclined.

The intern left to see what was awaiting him in the next cubicle and So What, Dot threw a blanket over Jody the O.D. as he slept it all off, peacefully as a baby. Then Dot got an idea. This guy and his antics had plagued her since she was a novice nurse. And besides, the place could use a little comic relief tonight. She turned around and drew the blanket up over Jody the O.D.'s face, like a corpse. Then she got another great idea. She filled out a morgue tag, which just happened to be lying around and tied it to his big toe. This might teach him a lesson or two.

Courtney was standing in the doorway of the cubicle as Dot turned around to leave. She was shaking her head and smiling. "Great sense of humor, DOT" she said as she turned to leave with her friend. "Maybe he won't be so quick to come back after this."

62

That's when they heard J.J. on the phone with the nurses on the eighth floor, playing "Doctor" again.

"What do you mean, the x-ray hasn't been done yet?! I ordered the x-ray hours ago! What the hell is going on up there?"

Apparently the nurse on the other end was informing J.J. that an hour ago, the patient was still in the ER.

"I don't give a rat's ass!" was his official and professional reply. "Get that x-ray done! I don't care how much the patient complains!"

An orderly was called 'stat' to Eight West and when J.J. heard the page over the loudspeaker, he smiled proudly to himself. His mother would be proud of the kind of power her son the D.O. had in this place.

The orderly arrived as soon as possible to the eighth floor and prepared to push the woman, bed and all, down to the x-ray department. Apparently what little effect the drugs had had, was wearing off quickly. First she told the orderly that she absolutely refused to be moved onto the gurney. The orderly told her kindly that he would take her down to x-ray in the bed, since she was in traction. Then she wanted to know how he thought he, alone, was going to push such a big heavy bed. Without saying a word, he simply rolled up the sleeve of his shirt and flexed some of the most impressive biceps the old woman had seen in a lot of years. Then, and only then, did she comply with the young orderly who unlocked the wheels of the bed and began rolling her past the nurses station and out toward the elevators. The charge nurse rolled her eyes as the orderly passed with the old lady in the bed. The old lady caught him smiling and demanded to know what was so funny.

She lectured him all the way to the elevator about how this was a hospital. That hospitals were full of sick people who were in pain and that no one had any right to be smiling in a hospital. "Yes, Ma'am" answered the exasperated orderly as he pounded several times on the button for the elevator to come. Everyone always seemed to think that punching that button would somehow make the elevator come faster. But, this orderly was punching it purely out of frustration, as he tried to ignore the obnoxious patient, with whom he would have to endure the elevator ride.

After what seemed like a good ten minutes of waiting and listening to this old lady complain about everything and everybody, he heard the "ding" sound above the doorway and the rickety old doors slid open. The orderly was already positioned at the foot of the bed to just push the bed onto what looked like a darkened car. So what else is new, he thought as he figured that the lights were out in the elevator car and that now he would have to listen to another tirade from her about why the lights weren't working.

He took a deep breath and pushed the traction-laden bed with all his might, into the elevator. He would never forget the sights and sounds that followed that one big push.

The woman screamed a terrified scream that echoed off the walls of the elevator shaft, then faded as she fell in her bed, through the shaft, from the eighth floor, to the ground floor. There had been no elevator car there when the doors had slid open. No wonder it had been so dark in there.

The Emergency Room, which was located on the ground floor right near those elevators, was immediately notified of what had just happened and the crash cart and code team were dispensed to the scene. But the elevator wouldn't open. The maintenance department, much to their amazement, was called stat. They worked feverishly on getting the doors open, but it was ominously quiet behind those doors. Especially for a lady who liked to swear and complain so much.

At long last, the doors were opened and the patient was found hanging by her Bucks Traction from the bed. The team cut the traction ropes and expertly pulled her from beside the bed, but to no avail. The woman was dead. The code team couldn't get her back.

As usual, Dot recognized the fruitlessness of all the effort, way before anyone else did. She turned to Courtney, as if she were going to say something profound. She did.

"Better call x-ray and tell them to make it a portable."

Chapter Fourteen

Explanations

"Goddammit! What kind of illegal alien do you have cooking back there this week?" bellowed Mike Murphy in an angrier than usual tone.

"Who'd ya expect? Julia Childs?" answered Sam Manetti sarcastically. He knew Mike was going through a rough time, but he was getting a little tired of the constant complaints and arrogance from him.

"Well, I know I asked for my roast beef sandwich medium **rare**, but I did expect that whoever ya got working' back there this week would at least pass a match under it, Goddammit!"

Everyone in Nine-One-One ignored Mike Murphy's angry tirade. They were used to it by now. Ever since the homicide of his only daughter, they had seen a marked increase in his insolence, but they had paid it no mind. After all, it wasn't something you wouldn't expect from Mike Murphy. Mike pushed his stool away from the bar rather dramatically, making an almost ear-splitting noise as the stool scraped across the wooden floor under his burly frame.

"Mike, you go in there and upset one more a' my cooks and I'm gonna eighty-six you from here. You've made two cooks quit on me already in one week! I can't afford to keep losing cooks cause you're in a bad mood!"

"Yeah, it must be real rough finding a new, starving illegal alien looking for a job around here" Frank muttered, as he pulled his stool back in. "Why don't ya do somethin' brilliant, like see if they can cook, before you hire them?" he added, sarcasm dripping from his mouth along with the juice from the rare roast beef.

"You know, Mike, if I were you, I'd be real careful. A few of these cooks that you roughed up back in the kitchen over the quality of your roast beef sandwiches wanted to press charges" Sam Manetti warned. "You oughta be mighty grateful that I talked them outta it."

"Yeah. That'll be the day some illegal alien is stupid enough to file a complaint against a cop" Mike smirked arrogantly.

"They're not all illegal aliens" Sam countered.

"Well, the least you could do is take this sandwich back to him and tell him to **cook** the meat this time. This is America. We only eat animals **after** they're dead."

Courtney, who was sitting beside the Padre, who was sitting beside Mike Murphy looked questioningly at the priest. "I think I liked him better when he was going through his silent stage" she whispered, both eyes guardedly on Mike.

"This is progress" said the Padre, taking a swig of beer and staring straight ahead.

"You call this progress?" she said a bit confounded. "I'd hate to see him in regression."

The good Padre smiled before addressing her very legitimate remarks. "Surely, being a nurse, you know about the five stages of grieving? I thought you people studied all that kind of stuff?"

"Well, yes we do, but I never heard of harassing short order cooks till they quit described as a normal stage of grieving" Courtney said in all seriousness.

"Sure you did. It's the second stage. Anger. The first stage is denial and isolation." The Padre was smiling at her again. "Mike went through the first stage when he drank himself into a stupor every night, then Gantz and I had to carry him up to a bed upstairs. For a while there, Room #10 was his home."

"I remember it well" Courtney answered.

"Well all that drinking and sleeping it off upstairs was his way of denying what had happened and of isolating himself from the world. Now he's in stage two. Anger. He's progressing."

"Well, while he's progressing, I hope he doesn't get fired. I heard he actually went back there and put the cook up against the wall for giving him the wrong kind of salad dressing. If enough of these people complain, he's going to have some explaining to do.

"It'll all work out" Father Murphy said confidently as he took a swallow of beer.

"Just what makes you so sure?" Courtney wanted to know.

"Well, it's like you. I'm sure you never dreamt you'd be able to survive emotionally without your husband. But here it is, almost a year, and you're surviving. I mean, you might have your rough days, but all in all, you're a highly functioning human being. You're a productive member of society and eventually, the pain will go away and you'll come back to life again. Real life, I mean."

"I'm not so sure sometimes" she said softly, not wanting any arguments.

"I am. Trust me. You've handled yourself like a pro, Courtney Quinn."

"It just looks that way because I'm a girl" Courtney said sincerely into her beer.

Father's curiosity was piqued. "What do you mean by that?"

"Well, maybe I need to go through all those stages of grieving too. But if I started lashing out at people and beating up cooks because my roast beef was too rare, they'd have me locked up on the Psychiatric ward of City Hospital. But, Mike, or any man for that matter, can go around picking fights and acting violently over stupid stuff, and nobody thinks twice about it. They just say he's going through a rough time."

Father Murphy looked long and silently at Courtney. "I know" he finally said. "It's not an easy world to be a man or a woman. But you know what?"

"What?"

"Grief is a lot like when there's a hurricane or a serious Nor'easter and the tide starts coming in here and rising. If you watch for it to recede, it seems like it never will. But if you turn your attention to something else, all of a sudden you realize that the water's going down. And like grief, it fades, it recedes slowly, but it does eventually recede. And I promise you, Courtney Quinn, whatever methods you or Mike decide to use to cope with your grief, even if they're different as night and day, the pain **will** go away. Maybe not completely, but other things will come into your life to fill the holes. The key is to hang in there, until that happens."

"But sometimes I feel like taking my ball and going home, Father. I don't want to play this game any more."

"Take a look at Mike over there. You think he wants to go on playing ball? That's the point. You really don't have a choice. You have to play ball or die yourself."

"Sometimes that doesn't seem like an altogether bad idea." Courtney said sadly.

"What, dying? Dying because you're in so much pain?"

"Yes" answered Courtney truthfully.

Father Murphy stared long and hard at her. "Listen to me Courtney Quinn. We, all of us, are each like a rare and exotic flower that has to open at it's own rate. Some things slow down our progress, some things speed it up. But always, especially when we're sent a great deal of pain to deal with, we are growing and blossoming in our own unique way around the pain and the obstacles." Then he looked at her haunted face and added, "I know this doesn't sound very profound, but I really have to visit the men's room right now. Will you excuse me, please?"

Courtney's face lost the haunted expression and she broke into a smile. "I know what you mean. Go right ahead" she said.

Frank Stoner was sitting on the other side of her and beside him sat Fred Gantz and So What, Dot. Howitzer Fred was whining and basically crying in his beer about how unhappy be was in his job, as Dot lent a sympathetic ear.

"I been on the force almost a year now and I could count the times I've seen any real action on one hand. Usually, the most exciting thing that happens on an average night, is that someone calls us cause they notice this horrendous smell and then realize they haven't seen their next door neighbor in a while. So we go and break the door down, and we always find some poor slob, usually sitting on a toilet or doing a perfect three-point stance after falling off the toilet, and they're dead from a heart attack or something. And the **smell** is horrendous! Why do dead people have to smell so bad, Dot?"

"Well, how long do you suppose they're been dead by the time you find them?" Dot asked clinically.

"A few days, I quess" answered Fred innocently.

"Well, no wonder. At least when **we** get dead bodies, they're still warm."

Courtney didn't feel like listening to this morose conversation much longer, but since Stoner the Loner was sitting next to her, she knew she wasn't going to be having any profound conversations. At least not till the Padre came back from the men's room. She was surprised though, that Frank Stoner and

Boris had ventured to sit at the bar. After all, it was snowing out, but it was low tide and the floor was dry. Besides, Gantz was beginning to whine so loud, Courtney didn't really have much choice but to listen to his long list of complaints.

"And besides," Fred was saying, "why do all these old people end up dying on the toilet? I mean, what is so deadly about a toilet when you get up into your eighties? Yet, that's where we find the vast majority of them. Why is that Dot?"

"It's something called the vaso-vagal response" she answered matter-of-factly.

"The what-o, what- response?" Gantz drilled Dot.

But Dot, realizing the futility of explaining anything medical to Gantz, especially after he'd had a few beers, decided to bring it right down to basics. "There's a big nerve inside the rectum, Gantz, and let's just say the ass bone's connected to the heart bone, so when anything stimulates that nerve in the rectum, I mean like the person taking a strenuous dump, it causes the heart to short out and they die."

Gantz seemed perfectly satisfied with that answer. And Courtney couldn't help laughing at the simple truth behind it. But Gantz wasn't done whining. He often got like this after a few beers. Mike Murphy started fights and Fred Gantz started whining about his job. "You know what the most exciting thing that happened to us tonight was?" he asked Dot, assuming that she would be sitting on pins and needles waiting for his answer. "We get this call. It's a pregnant woman."

"Oh, you're not gonna tell that one, are ya?" called Mike Murphy across the barstools between them.

"Hell, yes!" answered Gantz, "It's a perfect example of how our training and talent are wasted on 99% of the calls we get" He went back to his story. "So this pregnant woman calls. Says she's due to have her baby any day now, but she thinks she's having it now cause the pain's so bad and she's requesting an ambulance. Mike and I are right in the area, so we get there before the First Aid does. She's sitting in a chair, all bent over in pain, holding her stomach. Her husband's out in the kitchen, boiling water, I don't know what for. Anyway, that First Aid gets there and Mike and I help lift her onto the stretcher. Just then, she lets rip the most hideous and repulsive fart I have ever witnessed. Then she says, "Oh, officers, I feel much better now. The pain is all gone." Fred turned to his audience and said, "Now, do you call **that** police work?"

"Just be glad it was only a fart" said So, What, Dot like the true veteran nurse she was.

Frank Stoner then turned to Courtney and said, "Do you mind if Boris sits up on this stool next to you? I think he's feeling a little left out down on the floor like that."

Courtney laughed and agreed to it. "Frank," she said rather boldly, "how come you're being so sociable lately? I've never seen you sit at the bar before."

"Yeah, well, I was working' up the nerve to ask the padre for a favor" Stoner explained, turning big, Cocker Spaniel eyes toward Father Murphy.

"I hope you're not gonna ask me to give Boris Communion again" the Padre said defensively. "I already told you I can't do that."

"No, no. Nothing like that" Stoner laughed, a little embarrassed. "I was gonna ask you to say a novena for a special intention of mine."

The Padre looked ling and hard at Stoner. "This wouldn't have anything to do with next Saturday afternoon, would it?" he asked suspiciously.

"You know me like a book" Stoner grinned. Then, turning to Courtney, he explained that next Saturday, Padre and some of the cops planned to spend the day in the casinos. It was their annual "Day of the Dice".

It was also the one year anniversary of Paul's death and Courtney was so caught up in that thought that she didn't hear Stoner inviting her and Dot to join them.

"Count me out" Dot said loudly, bringing Courtney back to the present moment. "I never win in those places, and I'm a very sore loser. Besides, I have to work Saturday."

"What about you, Courtney?" Fred Gantz called to her.

Courtney was torn for a moment. Spending a day in a gambling casino didn't seem like an appropriate way to spend the first anniversary of her husband's death. But then, what was appropriate? Spending the day alone, torturing herself with memories? Wouldn't it be better to be among friends and losing herself, at least momentarily, among the bells, lights and clinking of coins in those metal trays?

She smiled up at their expectant faces. "Just call me 'Lady Luck'" she said.

Chapter Fifteen

Finger Food

Gantz, Murphy, Stoner and the Padre had said they'd meet her around two o'clock in Caesar's. They said she'd probably find them hanging around the crap tables.

It was two thirty by the time Courtney was finally walking along the famous Atlantic City boardwalk. She didn't think they'd really mind her being a little late, especially if they were on a winning streak. In fact, the possibility of a winning streak, combined with the fact that there are no clocks anywhere inside the casinos, made her quite confident that her tardiness might easily go completely unnoticed.

Besides, it was one of those rare and exceptional days you sometimes get in December in New Jersey. A day that feels more like April. The sun was sharing an unusual amount of warmth and people were walking on the boardwalk with coats and sweatshirts tied around their waists. Courtney had had to fight with herself to go in the first place, but now she was glad she was here. Part of her had wanted to just not get out of bed and to lie wound missing Paul and hugging Zachary and maybe crying a stored up tear or two. But then, part of her wanted to find a way to forget the pain of what had started a year ago today. Part of her really wanted to come back to life again, to appreciate the good things that were still there, even though Paul wasn't. She was glad now that that was the part that had won.

As she walked along the boardwalk toward the casino, she couldn't help but notice how white the foam was as the ocean waves shattered against the waiting shore and rolled up as far as they could onto the beach. It was as if they were playing a game or having a contest, to see which foamy, bubbling wave could roll the farthest and surprise unsuspecting tourists strolling along the sand, expecting to keep their feet dry.

Seagulls were squawking and following the fishing boats that were coming in, dive-bombing them for scraps. They glided effortlessly on currents of air that were invisible to the human eye. Others still, flew low, scavenging the waters for any leftovers from the fishing boats. Courtney was thinking about how ecology, especially ocean ecology, had been such a serious and volatile subject for years now, here on the Jersey Shore, but as she watched nature in progress, she marveled at how it took care of itself. She was awed by the way the ocean kept cleansing itself by the waves washing up on the beach and the waters being sifted through the sand. She loved how the seagulls cleaned up every spare scrap of food or garbage left floating in the water. And when the waters surface was picked clean by the eternally ravenous seagulls, and it was pulled back off the shore, newly sifted through the sand, the sun would seem to dance off of it, like a million glittering diamonds all the way out to the horizon.

And the salty air, that was her favorite part. There was something completely unique about the aroma of the mixture of the clean, salt air combined with the slightly damp scent of the old wooden boardwalk. It was a wonderful fragrance and on a bright, sun-shiny day like today, it made the whole atmosphere particularly mesmerizing.

Courtney Quinn put her face up to the gentle, winter sun, breathed deeply and listened to the mustic of the seagulls. Nature was a much misunderstood, underestimated and astounding thing. Courtney hoped that she would somehow learn to fashion herself after this great maestro. She hoped she could learn to let the sporadic waves of pain that swept through her heart, somehow be sifted and cleansed. She hoped that she could understand the high tides and the low tides of her life and learn to just find higher ground when it was time to sit out a storm.

She took her eyes from the millions of dancing diamonds on the ocean to look at her watch. It was almost three o'clock. She'd better get going, if she were going to spend the afternoon with those guys and try to forget her troubles for a while.

She approached the casino doors just as she noticed a particularly bold seagull, dive-bomb a lady with an ice cream cone. The ice cream was knocked onto the boardwalk and the seagull went about his business of happily chopping away at it, as the outraged woman looked around for someone, she didn't know who, to **do** something.

As Courtney pulled open the door to the casino, she couldn't help noticing that a simple, man-made door separated two entirely different worlds. Inside the casino it seemed almost pitch black compared to the dazzling sunshine she had just left. It took a moment or two for her eyes to adjust, but when they did, it was a different kind of light she saw. There were flashing lights on top of slot machines that winked and vacillated and drew your attention to the winners. Instead of the scree of seagulls, there was the sound of bells ringing and video-type musical tunes being played. There was the sound of metal coins splashing into metal trays and shrieks of delight as well as angry warnings and desperate pleas from not so lucky patrons talking to their machines. It was a completely artificial world, and yet it could be almost as mesmerizing as the one she had just left behind the door to the boardwalk.

Courtney found her way to the crap tables and was completely amused by the intensity of the players, the superstitious and compulsive rituals they went through before rolling the dice and the unfamiliar sayings she heard being shouted out as they rolled. She heard them shout things like "Yo, lev" or "hard eight" or "let it ride". It was a whole new language to her. In fact, it was a whole new, and somewhat intimidating, world to her. It was mostly men who were playing craps and yelling these foreign phrases to the dice. She spotted the group she was looking for, Gantz, Murphy, Stoner and the Padre, but she didn't dare approach. Gantz was rolling the dice and she felt certain that there would be some sort of superstitious blame put on her if he "sevened out" when she approached. So, she stood back and watched the game until Frank Stoner and the Padre both noticed her at the same time.

Gantz and Stoner were both puffing on big cigars and the fact that Stoner was actually smiling for once and looking sociable, even though Boris had not been allowed in with him, took Courtney by surprise. Then she noticed the pile of chips in front of the two men. There were several green ones and a few that looked black and white. And there were two or three orange ones. Courtney had no idea how much each color was worth, but she knew that in order for Frank Stoner to be smiling, they must be doing all right.

Father Murphy walked over to Courtney and greeted her with a smiling "Glad you could make it."

"Sorry I'm late," she apologized.

"You are?" Father Murphy said, only then rolling up his sleeve to see what time it was. "So you are" he said. "Just shows you how much fun we were having when we don't notice the absence of a beautiful young lady" he smiled.

"How are you all doing?" she asked, feeling a little awkward. She really wished So What, Dot didn't have to work today and could have come with them. But it had been mostly Dot who had convinced Courtney to join them today. She said sitting home thinking of the past was no way to get past it. She had said to think of this as a therapeutic treatment.

"Stoner and Gantz are doing great" smiled Father. "They each won over a thousand bucks. Mike's not having the same kind of luck though. He's getting irritable . . . and hungry. And when Mike gets either irritable **or** hungry, he gets ugly." Father was obviously familiar with this scene.

"What about you?" Courtney asked. "Are you winning?"

"I broke even" he said. "That means it's time for me to sit down and have a cocktail. After that, my luck usually goes in a positive direction. what do you say? Let's tell them we'll meet them in the cocktail lounge and maybe we can talk Mike into coming with us and getting something to eat. He always gambles better on a full stomach."

Father approached the group of men with his plan. As expected, Fred and Frank wanted to stay and continue gambling since they were both on a hot streak. Mike said he wanted to watch for a few minutes, but then he would meet Courtney and the Padre in the cocktail lounge. "My stomach is making more noise than a Puerto Rican in labor" he said.

The Padre expertly led the way through the crowd toward the cocktail lounge, which was a good thing since Courtney was all but hypnotized by the allure of the place. Every where she looked, it seemed there were ways to get money. There were cash machines, change booths, places to establish a line of credit, men and women roaming the floor with aprons full of change and even machines right next to the slot machines so that you could get change without having to lose your squatter's rights to your machine.

"Have you ever played, Courtney?" the Padre smiled at her as he noticed her looking a bit like Alice in Wonderland.

"No, I never have" she said, feeling both embarrassed and intimidated.

"Why don't you play a few hands of Poker on the quarter machines?" he suggested. "I won't take long and I'll show you how to play."

Courtney needed no more convincing than that. She got twenty dollars worth of quarters from a man with an apron full of change who wished her luck as she opened her hand to receive the two rolls of quarters. She had no idea how to play this video poker game, but the people who were playing it and making the bells ring and lights flash, didn't exactly look like rocket scientists. If they could do it, she certainly could learn to do it too.

At first, she was being a bit frugal, only wanting to bet two or three quarters at a time. But Father finally impressed upon her the foolishness of that type of strategy and soon she was betting the maximum bet. A whole five quarters each time. She lost most of the time. But just as she was running out of quarters and didn't think this game was much fun, she hit something called a straight flush. She loved the sound of the quarters that came pouring out and the bells that began to ring. A poker fanatic had been born.

"C'mon, let's go get a drink while you're ahead. You'll do even better when we come back, I promise."

And who was she to doubt him? He hadn't steered her wrong so far. Besides, they didn't want Mike to be looking for them, thinking they had forgotten him.

They sat at a table with a third chair that they were saving for Mike. Courtney ordered a gin and tonic and the Padre ordered a beer. She hadn't eaten anything substantial today, so she knew she shouldn't drink much until she at least put something in her stomach. But Mike didn't come right away, so they both had a second drink. When he finally did show up, he wasn't interested in drinking. He was interested only in gambling. His luck had suddenly changed for the better and he wouldn't have left the crap table except that he was so hungry.

"Listen, I'm gonna run out on the boardwalk and get a hamburger from one of those vendors. Then I'm goin' right back to the tables. Old Mikie is hot tonight!" he informed them.

"What about comps, Mike?" asked the padre. "If you guys are doing so well, you know they're gonna give you some comps. Why not wait and we can all have a nice meal in a fancy restaurant upstairs?"

"I'll eat later too. But I'm starving right now. Do me a favor and hold onto these chips for me, will ya?" he said as he dumped one orange and several black and white chips into the Padre's hand. "I don't want some local thug out there on the boardwalk tryin' to rob me while I eat my burger. I'll be back in a few minutes for it" and with that he was gone, making his way through the crowd toward the boardwalk.

"How much money is that?" asked Courtney. "I have no idea what the different color chips stand for."

73

The Padre smiled. "The orange one's worth a thousand."

"Dollars?" Courtney asked, incredulous.

"Yes. And the black and white ones are worth a hundred bucks a piece. The others are only worth five to twenty-five bucks. All in all, I'd say Mikie's making a comeback."

Courtney was quiet for a moment. "That's what I want to do someday," she said, the drinks going to her head. "I want to make a comeback."

"You haven't lost anything yet" said the Padre, not quite understanding what she was talking about.

"Not in here, maybe" she said through slightly misty eyes.

"Oh. _That_ kind of comeback. That's the toughest kind."

"I know. Believe me."

"Yeah. But at least you're out today, having a good time. I think that's very commendable. It would have been very easy for you to stay home and feel sorry for yourself."

"Don't give me too much credit. I almost did."

"But you didn't." Father's eyes grabbed hold of hers. "That's the important thing. You gathered up your strength and came out. You're gonna do fine."

"I hope you're right. I hope you'll be calling me the 'comeback queen' someday," she said, trying to add a little humor.

"I'm sure we will. You've got everything it takes to be a 'comeback queen'. You're young and healthy. You have a great profession. And you're not a quitter."

Courtney lowered her eyes. "Yes I am" she said.

"What? A quitter?" Father couldn't believe his ears.

"I quit nursing once. I got so fed up with being taken advantage of by the administration, that I quit."

"I know. I heard about it." Father said with a note of both pride and humor in his voice. "Didn't I hear that you transferred to the housekeeping department, just to embarrass the hospital into improving conditions for nursing?"

"Yup. That was me."

"That was great. So what brought you back to nursing? Last I heard you were doing the talk show circuit and giving speeches to nursing organizations about how to bring about change in the nursing profession."

"I was. But then when Paul was killed, that kind of changed everything. I needed to have a routine again. And I wanted to be out of the house at night. Nights are the hardest time for me. But at least I have Zachary, our dog. He's great company."

"Guess that's why they call them 'Man's best friend'. But tell me something. How does it feel to be back in nursing again? Aren't all the old frustrations still there? And don't you still have the same gripes against the administrators? Or is City Hospital a little better than most, as hospitals go?"

Courtney laughed. "No, all hospitals are pretty much the same as far as the politics go. But working in the E.R. keeps me pretty far away from administration. At least farther away than I would be if I were working up on the floors. I don't know how I ever did it. I don't know how anybody does it, working on those floors and always being treated like a second class citizen. Not much has really changed yet. It will someday, but it's time just hasn't come yet, I suppose."

"And what about the personal side of Courtney Quinn?" Father asked compassionately. "How is **she** doing?"

Courtney took a deep breath before answering. "Sometimes, I think, Yeah, O.K. I'm gonna be O.K. I think I'm gonna live. But then there are days when I think I'll never get through even the next hour without Paul. And that I'll never be able to leave the past behind and start any new relationships."

"Easy, Courtney" Father advised. "It hasn't been that long. Cut yourself a break. Don't let anyone tell you how far you should be right now. We all have to go at a rate that is unique to us. Trust the process. It's on your side."

Courtney thought for a moment. "I'm really glad you didn't go getting all religious on me, Padre. I gave up on formal religion years ago. Then when Paul died, I gave up on a belief in anything.

"I thought you were Catholic?" the Padre asked.

"You're right. I was."

He smiled gently. "Once a Catholic, always a Catholic" he said teasingly. "Just like nurses. Once a nurse, always a nurse."

"That's not true" Courtney said completely seriously. "In fact, I see a big parallel between nursing and Catholicism."

"Well, don't keep me in suspense" he said.

"Well, I think that Catholicism, like nursing, is something you outgrow . . . especially after life throws you a few curve balls and you start thinking for yourself instead of blindly believing everything that everyone shoves down your throat."

The Padre looked at her knowingly. He knew not to try to convince her of the faith he knew she had, even if she was too blinded by her pain to see it right now. No, this was definitely not the time for religious discussion.

Then it occurred to him that Mike Murphy still had not come back from getting his hamburger on the boardwalk. He knew how much Mike loved to play craps, especially when he was winning. Father had an uneasy feeling.

"Where do you suppose Mike is?" Courtney said as if reading his mind. "I felt sure he'd be back by now."

"Me too" answered the Padre. "I'm a little worried. Maybe we should take a stroll out there and see if he's all right. It's still light out. We should be able to find him."

Courtney and the Padre got up, both of them feeling their drinks on their empty stomachs. They made their way to the doors and walked out into the dimming daylight.

The boardwalk was full of people strolling and enjoying the extremely mild December day. They were like camels, trying to store it all up in a hump somewhere for the long, cold barren days that everyone knew lay ahead. Courtney couldn't help but notice the Padre's handsome features as the dim gold of the setting sun threw flattering hues across his face. She couldn't help wondering why such a handsome and delightful man like this would ever join the priesthood.

Father Murphy couldn't resist stealing a glance at Courtney's perfect and creamy complexion as the last golden rays of the sun reflected in her blue, blue eyes and slow-danced on the golden brown hues of her hair. He couldn't help but wonder how long it would take before she would allow her wounds to be healed and to let someone in again.

They both noticed the crowd gathered around the sandwich vendor's little cart at the same time. Apparently someone was bleeding quite profusely and an ambulance was needed. As they got closer, they realized that it was Mike Murphy standing in the middle of the crowd and applying tremendous pressure with a blood-soaked handkerchief to what was left of his index finger. Apparently, Mike had not been happy with the stingy piece of onion the vendor had put on his burger. He had then, in his usual ornery and arrogant manner with cooks lately, insisted that he cut his own slice of onion. The knife was a sharp one and when Mike began to dramatically cut **his** idea of a healthy slice of onion, he missed and cut the top half of his index finger off. Everyone was horrified, but everyone also stood and stared at the yelping off-duty policeman as he held his stump of a finger between his legs and applied pressure with all his might. "Don't just stand there, you morons! Get me an ambulance!" he was demanding. The crowd thought he was a mad man.

Just then, a seagull swooped down, and with perfect aim and finesse, clutched the remains of Mike's amputated finger in his seagull jaws and flew away with it, ready for a seagull feast.

"Son of a bitch!" Mike shrieked. "That bandit with feathers has got my finger!"

With that, Mike took off down the boardwalk, screaming like a maniac and chasing the feathered filcher. Courtney and the Padre both called, "Mike, No!" but to no avail. They knew he needed medical care, more than he needed the amputated end of his finger. And besides, what were that chances of capturing a seagull who was preparing to dine on 'finger food' on an Atlantic City rooftop somewhere. But both Courtney and the Padre underestimated how far Mike was willing to go to get his finger back. They chased after him, but Mike was way out in front. He still had his eye on the culprit and would have picked him out of a line up of twenty similar looking seagulls.

The seagull, sensing that he was being chased, by a crazy man no less, landed atop one of the lamp posts that lined the boardwalk. It was almost as if he were teasing Mike and enjoying every minute of the 'upper hand' that he literally had.

Courtney and the Padre were horrified when they saw Mike bend over and pull his off duty gun from its ankle strap. Once again, they yelled in unison, "Mike! No!" but to no avail.

Two shots rang out. Feathers flew, then trickled down softly onto the boardwalk, and the big bird fell to the ground with a thud . . . with Mike's finger still clamped firmly in its jaw.

By this time, the ambulance had arrived and Mike insisted on bringing the dead seagull to the hospital with him, the way a person tries to capture the rabid dog that bit them, just in case there were any other kind of contamination that he should be aware of.

"Courtney, why don't you go in the ambulance with him and I'll go let Gantz and Stoner know what happened. Then we'll meet you over at the hospital." Father Murphy said.

"Of course" Courtney said as she climbed in the back of the ambulance with a grateful, but reluctant to show it Mike Murphy. As the paramedics were closing the back doors to the ambulance, the Padre heard Courtney add, "Just as long as he doesn't make me sit next to that dead seagull."

Chapter 16

Cop Turned Patient

City Hospital's Emergency Room, as usual, was already bustling with activity when Mike Murphy was pushed through the ambulance entrance on a stretcher. Courtney Quinn walked quickly beside him, keeping pace with the paramedics.

They had finally been able to control the bleeding during the short ambulance ride, and the stump of a finger was wrapped heavily in a sterile, pressure dressing. Next to Mike on the stretcher, laid a dead seagull with two bullet wounds in the thorax. Mike refused to let the felon, even though it was a dead felon, out of his sight. Besides, he was rather proud of what a good shot he had been. He never could have done that in target practice. With a severe injury to one hand, no less.

So What, Dot saw him roll by and go into cubicle seven, but she couldn't leave the patient she was with. The patient was clinically dead, which put him right at the top of the priority list. And mostly, it was J.J.'s fault that the guy's heart had stopped, which put J.J. right at the top of the lawyer's list.

What had happened was that the forty-eight year old patient had come in complaining of abdominal pain. The pain seemed vague, but no one could put a finger on what was going on inside the guy's abdomen. He just didn't seem to be in enough pain or to be "sick" enough to have what they called a "hot abdomen", which was a term they used when someone had an acute problem in the belly and would probably end up in the operating room. Nor did the patient have any rebound tenderness, meaning that it you pressed in on the abdomen in the area where he said it hurt, then suddenly let go, the patient would have severe pain. It was difficult to examine the patient's abdomen because he was so obese, and carried most of his weight in his rotund abdomen. The decision had been made to just sit and wait for a while. If it were a hot abdomen, like a appendicitis or something, the symptoms would have to get worse. More than likely, the medical team was thinking it might only be indigestion.

They had put in what is called a "Heparin Lock". It is a small needle with a sort of rubber plug on the end that sticks out of the vein, thus allowing intravenous medication to be given as many times as necessary without ever having to stick the patient again. It should probably have won some kind of honor as one of the most humane inventions of the hospital world. The only thing you had to be careful to do, was to be sure that you "flushed" the medication through with a normal saline solution after giving it. Otherwise, the medication would just sit inside the heparin lock and not get into the bloodstream.

Things had been going just swimmingly until J.J. decided that the guy was complaining too much and needed something to quiet him down. He made two mistakes. The first one was playing "doctor" and deciding to give the patient pain medication that could possibly mask the symptoms of a more serious illness before the general surgeons had a chance to examine the patient. The second mistake he made was that he decided to play "nurse" and administered the pain medication himself. And since he was anxious to prove that he knew what he was doing, he decided to do the nurse's job, not only by injecting the pain medication, but also by "flushing" the heparin lock. But he used the wrong "Flush". There were two packages of look-alike cartridges sitting side be side. One package contained saline flushes, the other contained injections of Morphine. Naturally, J.J. saw no obvious difference between the two and picked up the one with Morphine in it. He slipped it expertly into the heparin lock in the complaining man's vein and the man stopped complaining as soon as the Morphine started flowing through his veins. In fact, he stopped breathing too.

At first no one could figure out what happened, but first thing's first. A code was called and J.J. and the surgical resident who had just come down to examine the patient and to admit him to the surgical service for observation, began CPR on the unsuspecting and now unconscious patient. Once again, J.J. got stuck with the mouth-to-mouth part with his Maalox layered, white lips, but at least this time there was an ambu bag within reach. The surgical resident was doing chest compressions and both men were shouting between breaths and compressions for the "Goddamn code team".

During this time, it occurred to J.J. that when they revived this guy, he didn't want to have anything to do with him. In his professional opinion, the patient belonged on the general surgery service. It didn't look good for a patient to come into an Emergency Room complaining of a "stomach ache" and then die. No, the priority here, after resuscitating this guy, would be to transfer the whole problem to another service. Preferably, the general surgical service.

Dot was standing there with the guy's chart, looking for something they may have missed. Was the guy a diabetic? Did he have any history of heart disease? What? What could have caused this?

"Dot!" J.J. yelled between forced breaths from the ambu bag, "Take a verbal order. Write an order on the chart to transfer this guy to general surgery!" He gave the man another quick breath.

"That's not fair!" shouted the surgical resident as he pumped so hard on the patient's massive chest that ribs could be heard cracking from across the room. "I refuse to accept him on our service! We haven't even examined him yet!"

"Tough!" barked back J.J., his lips now not only white from the constant swigs of Maalox, but also from the terror of realizing he may have just killed a patient, though just how, he didn't know. It still hadn't occurred to him what had

79

happened. J.J. quickly gave the patient another breath and yelled to Dot again, "go ahead, write it on his chart! Transfer this guy to the surgical service!"

"J.J." Dot yelled back. "You know better than that! I can't write an order on a dead patient!"

The surgical resident laughed as another rib splintered beneath his beefy hands. "I told you, J.J., this one's all yours. Just because you don't want to mess up your statistics, doesn't mean we're gonna let him mess up ours. He stays on your service, at least till this crisis is over!"

The anesthesia resident arrived, but just as he began intubating the patient, a light bulb went on in J.J.'s brain. "Let me see that package of saline cartridges" he said softly to Dot. He read the label that clearly said, "Morphine".

"Oh shit" he said, loud enough to be heard by some of the code team. Some of them looked up at him. After having spent enough years on the code team, they knew there was an important meaning behind the tone used when J.J., and many others before him, had said, "Oh, shit".

J.J. looked at the team quiltily and said, "Better give him an amp or two of Narcan. I think the problem is I just overdosed him on I.V. Morphine when I flushed his heparin lock."

The Narcan was given and the patient came around. Of course, he had to be admitted for the broken ribs now. But at least his abdominal pain was gone, though some felt that was just because his ribs hurt **more.**

As soon as the man transferred out to the Intensive Care Unit, just for overnight observation, Dot began to clean up the mess they had made during the code and restocked the cart so that it would be ready for the next one. Then she hurriedly made her way to cubicle seven, to see Mike Murphy. One look at him coming through the door and her trained eye knew that there was nothing life threateningly wrong with him. But she'd had to stay with the patient with the Morphine overdose before she could run in and see Mike.

When she pulled open the curtain to enter the cubicle, there was Mike, deliberately avoiding looking at the stump of a finger on his left hand and holding the dead seagull in a deathgrip, with his good hand. Dot laughed. "Who should we treat first, you or that poor seagull? The seagull looks like he's in a lot worse shape, to tell you the truth."

Mike didn't even crack a smile. "The son of a bitch tried to make a meal of my finger" he said, still angry.

"Haven't any of the docs been back here to see you yet?" she asked calmly, as she expertly lifted the pressure dressing the paramedics had applied and peered into the nasty wound.

"Yeah, there was a code going on, otherwise, you know we'd have gotten to you first" she said a bit apologetically. "How's the pain?" she asked.

"I ain't got none" he answered in his best, macho cop attitude.

That was the only hard part about taking care of cops as patients. They were always so reluctant to show that they had any human frailties, like pain or emotions. They didn't like to think they were like anyone else as far as weaknesses or vulnerabilities go. They liked to think they didn't feel pain. They liked to hope they'd never have to. She guessed it was an attitude that came with the job. They didn't want to have to be afraid of what **might** happen.

"O.K., Mike, let's take a look here" she said as she began unwrapping the remaindeer of the bandage and getting it ready to be cleansed and examined by the doctor. "J.J. will be in here in just a minute. He's just washing up".

"Oh, that's reassuring" chortled Mike.

"He's not as bad as some" Dot said with a smile. "Seriously, he works hard and he'll take good care of you. I'll see to that" she said reassuringly. "Besides, he'll only look at you down here. You know you'll probably go to the O.R. to try to replant the finger. You'll have the hand specialists for your surgery."

"Thank God."

"Speaking of the finger" Dot said, distracting him as she poured an entire bottle of Hydrogen Peroxide over the wound, "It's not still in the seagull's mouth is it?"

"No, the paramedics took it out and put it in a bag of ice."

That's when J.J. walked in, examined him and called the hand surgeons to take a look. Mike was informed that they were preparing an operating room for him now and that they'd be taking him as soon as they were ready. They said that all things considered, the amputated piece of the finger was in pretty good shape and that the seagull really hadn't mangled it at all. He hadn't been such a bad seagull after all.

Dot came back in to help Mike remove his clothing and to witness his signature on the surgical consent the doctors had wanted him to sign. But Dot refused to come near him until he let go of that dead seagull and let her have an orderly take it away. Mike grudgingly complied and Dot began to help him get undressed and to put on a patient gown, all with the gentlest and most expert touch he had known. He had no doubt that she would protect his now throbbing stump of a finger and he trusted her completely.

He let go of the dead bird and the orderly took it out. "I don't know why I got so mad at that seagull," he said, "he was just being a normal seagull. He saw a meal and he went for it. It really wasn't his fault."

"You just needed **something** to be angry with" said So What, Dot, completely understanding the situation.

"Yeah, but now there's gonna be hell to pay for using my gun like that. I've already been warned about the fights I been having with them short order cooks down at Nine-One-One. The Captain ain't exactly gonna be pleased with me when he hears I used my off duty gun to shoot a seagull in the middle of the crowded boardwalk."

So What, Dot was just draping the gown over Mike's left arm, not even daring to take a chance on hurting him by pulling his arm through the sleeve. "Mike" she said, in a tone he had never heard from her before, "It's O.K., you're a human being. You're allowed to make mistakes. If I'd been through what you've been through, I'd be mad at more than seagulls and short order cooks. I'd be mad at the world."

"I am."

"I know. I guess what I'm trying to tell you is that you're allowed to be. We're all your friends down at Nine-One-One. We understand, no matter who else doesn't."

Mike was silent. He was truly touched by this sudden show of gentleness from So What, Dot. And he believed her. He knew that they really **were** his friends down at Nine-One-One. Why else would they have put up with him the way they had? O.K., maybe he had suffered the worst calamity and the deepest pain a human being could know, but he also had the best friends in the world. Friends who shared his pain, who tried to help, even if it was only in a clumsy way sometimes. They were his friends and he couldn't keep punishing them with all of his pent up rage and bitterness toward the man who had just taken his daughter from him. No, the answer was to just find the slimeball who had hurt her like that and who had ripped out a piece of his very soul that could never be replaced. And when, not if, but **when** Mike Murphy found that slimeball, he would give him a lesson in pain unlike any that had ever been suffered by a human being. And only then, would he do the pig the favor of killing him. But he knew at this moment, that he would try to stop taking his anger out on these good people who were his friends.

Dot noticed the moisture in Mike's eyes as he avoided her glance by staring down at the floor. Dot knew he would rather die than let anyone see him in so human a condition. She knew it was time for a little rough, maybe even a little sick comic relief.

"Here" she said, as she handed him the surgical consent and pen. "Sign this paper. It's just a document saying that if we kill you on the operating table, it's not our fault."

Mike smirked in spite of himself. Dot was one hell of a nurse. And she was one hell of a human being too.

The gurney arrived to take Mike to the operating room and, like most cops, he refused the hands that offered to help him and slid himself over onto the stretcher. When the orderly wheeled him out into the corridor, there was Fred Gantz, Frank Stoner, Courtney and the Padre, all waiting to see him before going to the OR.

They all took a few steps toward the gurney and wished him luck. Stoner waved a couple thousand dollar bills in the air that he had won at the crap table while Mike was shooting seagulls.

"Don't worry, Murphy we're gonna get you the best private duty nurses money can buy," Frank Stoner said around the cigar that was still in his mouth.

"Yeah, we'll make sure she has a great ass and big ti. . . "He fell silent for a moment as Courtney and Dot eyed him. "Sorry girls. Just having a little fun" he leered.

"Yeah, we'll see how much fun you have in about twenty minutes from now," Dot said in a somewhat threatening tone, but he knew she was laughing behind it.

The orderly started to take off with the gurney, but Mike yelled out, "Hey, Padre! Padre! C'mere a minute." The gurney stopped. The Padre walked toward it. Mike looked up at him. "You think I oughta have Last Rites or something before I go?"

Father Murphy put his hand consolingly on Mike's wrist. "Mike, you're gonna be O.K. No one's gonna let anything happen to you. That seagull needed Last Rites more than you do."

"O.K., Padre" said Mike, satisfied with the Padre's answer. "But you better think up some kind of a prayer that they can reattach this finger or I'm gonna have to learn a whole new way of slicing onions."

Contrary to his expectations, going under general anesthesia was like falling into a cloud. A big soft, white, puffy one. He was rolling around on it, Feeling it's warmth engulf him and hold him like a big white sac of amniotic fluid again. He was a baby again, no, a fetus, and suddenly the heaviness, all the pain, all the scars were gone for a single moment as he heard a far away voice say, "O.K., he's out. Let's get started."

The surgery went splendidly. Mike Murphy could more than likely expect to not only keep his finger, but to probably recover a good 90% use of it. And since it was the non-dominant hand, it shouldn't really effect him in his work in any significant way.

He was wheeled into the Recovery Room, still garbling something about amniotic fluid and floating on clouds. His vital signs remained stable and the circulation of the finger looked good. The tip was nice and pink and it blanched when you tweaked the end of it, both good signs. The most important thing now was to keep the swelling down, and for that reason, his arm was raised up on pillows and supported by a splint that kept it from flopping down.

He was wheeled in this position onto the elevator and down to the surgical floor where he would be spending the next week or so. The orderly pushed his stretcher into the elevator and pushed the button for the second floor: general Surgery.

Courtney, Fred Gantz, Frank Stoner and the Padre were all seated in the little waiting room in front of the elevators on the second floor, waiting for their friend. Being as it was Christmas time, one of the many church groups in the area had its choir singing Christmas Carols for patients and visitors alike. It added a nice touch to the usually dismal atmosphere of the old, timeworn corridors. The group of friends waiting for Mike Murphy, were at least entertained during their wait.

Before Mike Murphy opened his eyes in the rickety old hospital elevator, he could have sworn he heard music. No, it sounded more like angels singing, Yeah, that was it. Oh Christ, he must have died in the operating room. The singing was getting closer and closer and he could have sworn it was "Silent Night" they were singing. He wondered if they sang it in English for everyone. More amazingly, he wondered how he ever ended up in Heaven. And then his heart sank as he realized he had let the Padre talk him out of receiving Last Rites.

83

The doors to the elevators opened suddenly and the sound of the St. James Choir burst forth so loudly, that it startled him. He opened his eyes and there was a crowd of friends around him. He knew them all. How did they get here? How could they have died too? And where was Devon? If Mike had gotten here, certainly, **she** must be here somewhere. It was the happiest moment of his life. He was convinced he was about to see his precious, precious daughter again, maybe this time without the knife wounds and the bandaged hands.

"How's the finger feel?" Padre asked him.

"Does it hurt much?" Courtney added. "Maybe we can get you something for it?"

"Hey, old man, you're lookin' pretty good there" said Frank Stoner, "maybe I should try some of whatever it is they gave you up there."

"Hey, Pal" said Fred Gantz. "Glad to see you looking so good."

Oh no. God no. He wasn't dead. He just wanted to be. Being dead had been wonderful. It felt so much better than being alive. No wonder no one ever comes back, he thought.

The St. James Choir moved in practiced unison down the hall, picking up the pace a bit with "We Wish You a Merry Christmas". Mike Murphy watched the hospital ceiling lights go by. He knew where he was now. And he knew what he had to do. So far his only clues were a thirty year old Caucasian male with a newly obtained tattoo of a rattle snake with a top hat printed in the web of his left hand, between the thumb and forefinger. Mike would find him. If it took the rest of his life, Mike would find him. He didn't care what it cost him, his job or even his life. His only consolation was that death hadn't been so bad. He hoped Devon was having the same kind of wonderful experience.

Chapter Seventeen

To the Rescue

They were only children. Both of them. The older one was a teen-aged girl. She was fourteen and had the newly budding body of a woman. And though she had all the confusing emotions and physical changes that puberty brings with it, she still had a child's mind and the classic innocence about such things.

The younger one was a boy. Her baby brother. He looked to be about five or six years old and was enjoying a game of stickball on the beach with his big sister. She didn't seem to mind babysitting for the little guy. It was the end of March and they had been blessed with an unseasonably warm day for so early in the Spring. So after having been cooped up inside electrically-heated houses and classrooms during the long, gray winter, it was utter joy to get outside in the sunshine. It wet their appetites for the summer that was not far behind.

Summers on the Jersey Shore are special, almost electric. People tend to go a little haywire. They behave something like a Biafran who suddenly finds himself in a gourmet restaurant. People who live in year-long warm climates cannot possibly appreciate what a special highlight the Summer weather brings to a winter-weary population. Living in a year-round warm climate, to the people of the Jersey Shore would be like every day being Christmas. After a while, no matter how great it is, it would lose its specialness, its excitement, its enchantment. Like little children on Christmas Eve, people on the Jersey Shore dream of the coming days of Summer and this somehow sustains them through the long, cold winters.

So on this almost Summer-like day, a fourteen year old girl and her six year old brother, were playing stickball on the beach still filled with winter driftwood.

Mike Murphy was walking the "boards" as they say in New Jersey, short for boardwalk. He was still out on disability due to the injury to his left forefinger, but as far as Mike was concerned, he was more than ready to go back to work. It had been about three months now since the injury, but the Captain had been adamant about Mike taking some time off.

The captain hadn't been as mad about the seagull shooting incident as everyone thought he would be. Everyone, including Mike, felt there was a good chance Mike could be dismissed from the police force for using such poor judgement that day. But the Captain had been a real human being about it. He didn't give Mike hell (which he was fully expecting and which he knew he deserved). The Captain had spoken in a very controlled and almost compassionate voice when Mike had come out of anesthesia that evening. He told Mike that this little incident didn't surprise him a bit. That it had been brewing for some time now. That it had been brewing since the night Mike's daughter had been murdered.

All in all, the captain had shown a surprisingly deep understanding of human psychology. He obviously understood the grieving process . . . and that Mike had not even begun this process. He'd told Mike that he was sorry he hadn't forced him to take time off after Devon was murdered. He said that these things take an awful lot of time alone to work out. And he seemed to know what he was talking about. Apparently the Captain had fought his own battles with grief, but was not about to share the details. He simply told Mike that this seagull stealing his finger incident might be a good thing. Mike really needed to take some time off and now he had no choice. He informed him of the amount of psychotherapy that was available to him through the department, and he encouraged him to go. Another definite sign that the Captain knew something about what Mike was going through.

Though he wouldn't have believed it at the time, Mike was glad now that he had been forced to take the time off. He walked along the "boards", breathing in the clean, salty air and watching the girl and her little brother playing stickball. He didn't blame them. The beach was such a relaxing place to be. In fact, he almost felt like going down on the sand and asking those two kids if he could join them. But then he saw something that struck him as odd. Call it suspicion. Call it police intuition. But Mike Murphy was suddenly getting an old, familiar, uneasy feeling in his gut.

He stood still as he watched a man of about thirty approach the little boy and ask him something. The child looked up at his sister with a question in his eyes. Mike couldn't be sure if the children knew this man. The man acted very familiar with them, but Mike sensed an uneasiness emanating from both children.

Out of habit, Mike stepped back so that he could observe the situation unnoticed. It was a strange thing, but even though it was the first beautiful Spring day they'd had, there was hardly anyone else around. Occasionally there would be a jogger going by on the boardwalk, but except for the man and the two children, the beach was deserted.

The girl seemed to be refusing a request by the man. She took her brother's hand protectively, but she wasn't fast enough. The man picked the boy up and put him on his shoulders, as if he were a friend or an uncle or somebody and he was going to give this frightened looking child a ride on his shoulders. The man ran down to the water's edge, bouncing the boy on his shoulders, "horsie style". The boy looked back at his sister with alarm in his eyes, and his sister, quite predictably, followed the man who held her brother captive.

Every instinct Mike, had, told him this was trouble, as he continued to watch from behind a deserted hot-dog vendor's stand. But he knew that "horsie rides" were not necessarily a criminal offense, and that if this guy was the bad news that Mike was certain he was, he would try something more in just a matter of minutes or seconds. There was no doubt that this guy was looking for trouble. But Mike needed more than a "horsie ride" to prove it. He spotted a public phone booth across the boardwalk and headed for it. He called the desk Sergeant and told him to send a car to the location where he was. He felt a showdown coming on. Then he went back to his post by the hot-dog stand and awaited his clue to intervene.

The man had waded into the water up to his knees now and he was shouting something to the girl. The girl was standing in ankle deep water herself, shoes and all. The man pulled the boy off his shoulders and menacingly dangled him just above the waves that were crashing at thigh height. It looked as though he was threatening to throw the little boy in the water. The child looked at his sister with terrified eyes and called her name. The stiff ocean breeze carried his panic stricken voice close enough to the boardwalk for Mike to hear it.

"Patsy! Patsy! Don't let him throw me in! I'm scared Patsy!"

Just as Mike took off like a shot toward the two terrified children he noticed the teen-aged girl crying and beginning to unbuckle the belt of her jeans. He sprouted wings as he flew through the sand. Now she unzipped the jeans and he could hear both children sobbing as the girl shouted in utter dread of what this man might do to her little brother, and in utter dread of what he was almost definitely going to do to her. "Wait!" she sobbed, "O.K. I'll do it! Don't hurt my brother!"

The man set the child down in ankle deep water just as Mike Murphy hurled his burly 225 lb. frame at him with the force of pro linebacker. The man fell into the wet sand and swirls of forty degree ocean water slapped their faces. Mike had caught him by surprise and so it was especially easy to wrestle him into a helpless position with the salty waves lapping at his face and torturously semi-drowning him.

But even if Mike hadn't caught the guy off guard, he still would have been easy prey. He had a slight and almost wimpy build. He hardly fought back at all, though it wouldn't have done him much good against a veteran cop like Mike Murphy. Still though, he wished he had his handcuffs with him Where was the radio car anyway?

Mike looked up at the two trembling children, as he let his victim continue to sputter and try to keep himself from the humiliation of drowning in two inches of water. The girl was clutching her brother protectively in her arms as they both watched in shock the scene before them. They didn't know who either of these men were, but they were certainly grateful that the second one had come along. Both children were visibly shivering and Mike knew it wasn't necessarily the cold.

"You kids stay where you are" Mike called to them in a protective voice. "There's a police car on its way to you now. Just sit tight for a few minutes."

Neither child showed any indication that they had heard their burly hero's instructions, but they timidly stood by and waited for the next turn of events.

Mike looked up and saw Fred Gantz and his new temporary partner pull up in the radio car and come running down the beach. Fred spotted the two shivering children, and realizing that Mike obviously had the situation under control, went back to the car to get blankets for the two wide-eyed children.

Mike was sitting on top of the still sputtering man who now was beginning to beg for mercy. Mike had the man's arm twisted up behind his back and as one of the foamy waves receded from his back, Mike noticed something very interesting. At first it just looked like an everyday tattoo, and Mike was thinking how this was the typical kind of guy who picked on people smaller than he, usually only women or children. These frail types always had to have tattoos for some reason. But as he looked at the tattoo more closely, his heart began to make strange fluttering movements in his chest. The tattoo was in the web of the left hand, between the thumb and forefinger. The color was vivid, as if it were newly obtained, and the design was a rattle snake with a top hat.

Gantz's new partner, Jeff Allen, was suddenly beside Mike, kneeling in the frothy waves and handcuffing the assailant. Jeff, being newly out of the academy, was only too thrilled to be involved in such a dramatic incident already. He looked up to Fred Gantz as an experienced veteran, which did wonders for old "Howitzer Head's" ego after having spent the last six months with Mike Murphy and all his derogatory and belittling comments about "rookies".

Gantz stayed with the two shocked and frightened children, wrapping them in blankets and speaking to them in reassuring tones. Jeff Allen easily cuffed the sputtering slimeball as Mike twisted the slimeball's arms painfully behind him. Mike hoped Jeff Allen wouldn't think it was always going to be this easy to subdue criminals. He didn't want him to get a false sense of security or anything.

Mike pulled the nearly drowned and now handcuffed, frail frame of a man up onto his feet with just one meaty hand. Jeff Allen thought perhaps Mike was being a little rough with a handcuffed prisoner, but he at least was know enough to keep his mouth shut around an old, cynical cop like Mike Murphy.

Mike still couldn't shake the fluttering in his chest that had now spread to his gut every time he looked at this weasel of a character. Mike knew from experience that the fluttering feeling was usually his gut, cop instinct trying to tell him something. Then he saw it. He stopped in his tracks and stared, unbelieving. This weasel was wearing a little half moon gold earring in one ear. the other half of the set Devon and Dennis had shared. The earring that Dennis had noted missing, the night of the murder.

"Mike, what's wrong?" asked Jeff with real concern as he looked at the odd but ominous look that was taking over Mike Murphy's face. "C'mon. Let's get this scum bucket in the slammer where he belongs."

Mike was silent. "He don't belong in no slammer" he finally answered, keeping the prisoner standing in the cold ocean water. If the prisoner thought he was scared before, he was petrified now. He watched the transformation of Mike Murphy's face go from that of a nasty, burly, off-duty cop, to that of a grotesque, almost Frankenstein-like mask.

With one swing of Mike's brawny, well-practiced arm, the prisoner found himself flying through the air with a jaw that surely was shattered and doing an almost admirable backflip into the frosty, beckoning ocean. It was an ocean that had taken many unsuspecting and undeserving lives during its history. But here was one body Mike wanted to see it take. Only drowning was too good for this weasel. Mike wanted him tortured first.

He pulled the gurgling prisoner to his feet and let him get just enough air into his lungs so that he thought he might soon be able to breathe again. Then Mike's fist connected with the already shattered jaw again sending the handcuffed prisoner into an almost perfect half gainer dive. It if hadn't been for the handcuffs, it might well have scored at least a nine.

"Murphy! For Christ's sakes! What're you crazy?!" Fred Gantz yelled from the beach. He ordered Jeff to stay with the two children and then Gantz, himself, waded quickly into the now waist deep water that Mike and the prisoner were standing in and grabbed Mike as the prisoner tried to stay afloat like a fish without fins. Gantz, though not as stocky as Mike, was in perfect physical shape and he grabbed Mike's fist to prevent it from striking another blow to the now dazed and disoriented prisoner. But Gantz's perfect physical condition was no match for the rage that burned inside Mike Murphy. Mike got in on more good shot, causing the prisoner to go under the waves one more time, but this time, he was unable to emerge.

"Gantz," Mike breathed heavily, "that's the guy. That's the guy who murdered Devon."

"What? Are you sure?" Gantz was shocked. Now he understood. the body of the prisoner rose feebly, one more time with the help of an oncoming ocean wave. But this time it was Gantz who landed a fist in the prisoner's face and left him unconscious and being dragged by the current into deeper water.

"Let's just let him go" Gantz suggested. "Let the slimeball drown."

"Drowning's too good for him" Mike answered as he deftly swam a couple of yards and grabbed the guy by the collar, dragging him to shore, with Fred Gantz supporting and helping his old partner every step of the way.

The prisoner would obviously have to be taken to the hospital instead of to the station. They radioed for a ambulance, but told them to take their time. When the paramedics got there, they knowingly asked no incriminating questions. Gantz murmured to them who the guy was and that he should get the "no frills" treatment.

They put the shivering and traumatized children into the radio car and took them down to the station. Their parents arrived within minutes of being notified of the whereabouts of their children. The mother entered the station with dry clothes in her arms and tears in her eyes. They wore a concerned and angry look. It was a scenario that had been played many times in the old station house. Both parents rushed to the back room where they were told the children were being questioned about what had taken place. Mike Murphy sat quietly on the side, listening to the children make sense of the events that he had witnessed.

It seems that man approached the young boy first and asked if he could play stickball with the children. The boy said he had to ask his sister first. The sister was leery of the man and wanted to get away from him without doing anything to ignite a problem. That's when the man tried to act all friendly by picking up the boy and giving him a "horsie ride" down to the ocean. He knew the girl would follow. When she did, he told her that if she didn't take her jeans off, he would drown her brother in the ocean. The boy started crying for her help and without giving it a moment's thought, the girl began to undo her jeans.

That's when Mike Murphy had intervened. Both children were trembling and crying as they told the story. Their mother wept openly and their father listened intently, grimacing and tightening the muscles in his jaw until he looked something like Mike had looked when he began to realize just who it was he had in custody. Only Mike Murphy could accurately interpret what was written on the father's face. Only Mike Murphy could understand the man's rage. And no one could even remotely begin to understand Mike Murphy's rage.

Chapter Eighteen

Revelations

"Yep, that's him all right" confirmed So What, Dot as she stared down mercilessly at the battered man who lay unconscious on the stretcher before her. "That's the guy we treated a few hours before Mike's daughter was brought in."

The detectives stared at one another. Though a witty lawyer may be able to convince a jury to doubt the credibility of Dot's ability to positively identify a man whose face was almost completely shattered, the detectives had no reason to doubt her conviction. Like most of the cops in the area, the two detectives had known Dot over a lot of years and through a lot of tragedies. And they had never known her to jump the gun or to be unsure either of herself or of her memory. She had an excellent mind for details and she never forgot a face . . . or a scar, or a tattoo for that matter. She would have made a great detective.

Dennis Donahue, Devon's widowed husband, was on his way down now to identify the earring in the guy's left ear. It was beginning to make sense now. Until now, the fact that the diamond stud in Devon's other ear hadn't been stolen had been a bit of a mystery. If the gold half moon had been stolen from one ear, it was easy to assume it was going to be sold for "drug money". So why not take the diamond too? But now it made a little more sense. Apparently the guy just liked the gold half moon and wanted to wear it himself.

The detectives spotted the ever-present coffee pot in the little room off the side and decided that would make a good place to wait for Dennis Donahue and whoever else they might want to talk to in order to find out for sure if this was the guy who killed Devon Murphy-Donahue. Besides, as usual, the Emergency Room was packed and the nurses and doctors had more than their share of things to do. The detectives decided to drink coffee and to stay out of the way as much as possible.

They sat by the doorway and got a free show of everything that was being brought in. There was the usual older men with chest pain, old ladies with hip pain, drunks with lacerations, young girls and belly pain, car accident victims with whiplash and all other kinds of injuries. It always amazed the detectives how the nurses and doctors could sift through the injuries and most of the time come up with the correct diagnosis and treatment.

Then they witnessed an ambulance pull up, a sixteen year old boy was wheeled past them on a stretcher. The two detectives had started a game of making bets on who had what, but both agreed that the teen-aged boy looked like a drug overdose. He was wheeled into a cubicle and curtains were quickly drawn around him as equipment was wheeled in and soon they heard the gut wrenching sounds of a stomach being pumped. The two detectives smiled at each other in satisfaction. Maybe they should have been doctors. They had been good diagnosticians at least once tonight.

They enjoyed sitting back and watching So What, Dot and Courtney Quinn prioritize patients and perform their duties like a practiced ballet. They scurried from cubicle to cubicle, bringing equipment, performing treatments and dropping off a reassuring word here and there when there was time.

The detectives knew it was just a matter of time before Mike Murphy would show up to gloat over the capture of his prisoner. Gloating would be O.K. and well deserved. But the detectives were a little uneasy about what else Mike Murphy was capable of doing to this guy. Not that they would have blamed him and not that the guy didn't deserve everything he got, but Mike's behavior was so unpredictable lately and the last thing they needed was a murder in the Emergency Room right under their noses. It wouldn't look good. They kept their eyes peeled for Mike Murphy's arrival. Besides, it hadn't been proven yet that this was the guy who had killed Devon Murphy-Donahue. Mike and Dot were the only ones who had no doubt, and they were only going on gut feelings and a few loose clues. Hardly enough to convict the guy. The best they could all hope for now, was for the parents of the assaulted children to press charges. At least that would keep the guy in custody and buy the detectives some time to find more convincing evidence that this was also a murderer they were dealing with. Worse than that, the murderer of a cop's daughter.

Dennis Donahue arrived with a face that showed absolutely no emotion. Word around town was that Dennis, like Devon's father, had done no grieving publicly, but his affect was completely flat, and like Mike Murphy, one suspected it would be just a matter of time before he would explode into tiny pieces somewhere. Fragments too tiny to ever put together again.

The detectives took Dennis to the cubicle that contained the earring they wanted him to look at. It was now an earring that just happened to be attached to a human being, not a human being with an earring.

Dennis' deadpan expression came to life when he spotted the little gold half moon on the swollen and bleeding ear of the badly contused and unconscious man on the stretcher. Now there were three people who were convinced that this was Devon's killer.

"Easy, now" said one of the detectives as he saw the fire ignite in Dennis Donahue's blue eyes. "It still may not be the same exact earring that we think it is. And the guy may have bought it from some other guy, some other junkie who was responsible for your wife's murder. We still have a lot to find out. We're got a lot of questions to ask this guy. Don't go jumping the gun."

But Dennis Donahue hadn't missed the tattoo in the web of the patient's left hand. He spoke slowly, but deliberately. "That nurse. McFadden, Dot McFadden was her name. She said they treated a guy in here a few hours before Devon was brought in. She said he had scratches all over him, like someone, probably a girl, was really fighting him for her life." Dennis looked down at the tattoo of the rattle snake with the top hat and added, "She said he

92

had a tattoo just like that one, in the same exact spot. She said they were a little suspicious of him and the kind of wounds he had, but they were really busy and they had no evidence to hold him on." Dennis Donahue hadn't forgotten a single detail of that devastating night.

The detective patted Dennis on the back. "Give us a chance, O.K.? It's not always as simple. Don't worry. We're pretty good at this. If this is our man, we'll find out and we'll nail him. It's just gonna take some time. That's all."

With that Mike Murphy came striding in the door. He walked up to Dennis and wordlessly shook hands with him, both men sharing a silent moment of grief that only they could understand. Both men were hurting all the time these days. But seeing one another somehow exacerbated the pain they each already thought had reached its highest limit. How wrong they were.

"Is the slimebucket conscious yet?" were Mike Murphy's first words to the detectives.

"Not yet. I think they're going to be taking him to the operating room to wire his jaw" one of the detectives said.

"So we can count on him being here a while, say at least a few days" said Mike hopefully.

"Oh yeah," came the answer. "You did a hell of a job on him. I think he'll be here for more than a few days" said the detective.

Dennis and Mike looked at each other and shared a contented smile, both men glad that at least Mike had gotten a few good shots in. Enough to keep this guy in one place until they could prove what they already knew.

So What, Dot then walked up to the group. "Well?" she said to Mike. "What's the story?"

"Not such a good one" Mike said a little despondently. They all looked at him a little surprised.

"Why don't we all go in the back room and have some coffee and you can tell us about it." Dot offered.

The group retreated to the back room where the ever present coffee pot sat waiting for them. They were all thinking it was too bad this wasn't like Nine-One-One where there surely would be a bottle of Irish Mist nearby, to help ease the tension of the story Mike was about to tell.

"How are those two kids doing?" asked one of the detectives, trying to ease into the delicate and possibly explosive discussion.

Dot began pouring coffee into styrofoam cups for everyone but herself and Mike . . . they had their own mugs. Dot's said "Love a nurse P.R.N.", hospital lingo meaning "as needed". Mike's said, "Admit nothing, deny everything and demand proof".

"The kids are gonna be all right, I guess" said Mike as he sipped the steaming coffee. "They're pretty shook up, but I'd hate to see the kind of shape they'd be in if I hadn't been there to stop that pig. By the way, did he have any I.D. on him?"

"Not a thing." said the detective, "But don't worry. We'll get you all the information we need as soon as he regains consciousness."

"Yeah, before I beat it out of him again." Mike answered viciously. "You guys better work fast when he wakes up, cause I certainly intend to."

"Let's get back to the kids" the detective said, trying to defuse Mike's rage. "Did they come up with any useful information?"

"Not really. They're too scared right now to be terribly coherent, but that ain't the worse part" Mike said, staring into his coffee mug. "I'm afraid we're gonna have a hell of a time getting the parents to press charges."

Dennis reacted for the first time. "What!?" he shouted, practically choking on his coffee. "How could they **not** press charges! That dirtball was about to rape their daughter - and maybe even their son!"

"It ain't that simple" Mike said with a practiced and level police tone in his voice. "They don't wanna see their kids go through what the defense attorneys for that slimebucket will most assuredly put them through."

"So they just want to turn this guy loose out on the streets where he can do it again? Maybe even to **their** kids again? I don't get it." Dennis was disgusted and frustrated and outraged. Welcome to the world of police work, Mike and the two detectives were all thinking.

"Dennis," one of the detectives began. "You don't know what those lawyers will put those kids through. Especially the teenage girl. They try to convince the jury that the girl was seducing him. Believe me. We've seen it a million times before. Most parents would feel their kids have been traumatized enough by something like this. They don't want to put the kids through anymore. They'd rather let them try to forget it and hope it never comes back to haunt them. Whereas, a trial could scar them worse than this guy already has. That's how these things work. It's really not surprising that the parents don't want to press charges."

"I can understand it to a degree" said So What, Dot, "but, I sure wish someone would talk them into it. I just know this guy is a bad apple. And I'd bet my bottom dollar on it that this is the guy you want for Devon's murder."

The room was silent for a few moments. Mike Murphy looked a little disappointed, but surprisingly concerned. And everyone could guess why. He had his own plans for this guy, whether or not a jury of his peers found him guilty. Mike had already brought him to trail in his own mind, found him guilty and sentenced him to death. Some way, some how. The man in cubicle seven was a doomed man. And everyone in the room knew it.

Dot finished her coffee and rose to her feet. She put a gentle but firm hand on Mike's shoulder. "I gotta get back to work" she said, "but I'll see if I can talk them into doing his jaw without anesthesia." No one in the room knew whether or not to take her seriously. She smiled at Mike and left the room.

When she found Courtney if was in cubicle eight with the sixteen year old suicide attempt from an overdose of sleeping pills. By now his stomach had been lavaged, or "pumped" and he was still groggy from the trauma he'd put himself through.

Courtney looked up and saw Dot standing in the cubicle behind her "What's going on?" she asked. "You need me for anything?"

94

"Nothing serious, but I could use some help restocking the code cart if you're not terribly busy" Dot answered.

They walked out of the cubicle together and toward the code cart. They began opening drawers, counting supplies and replacing them. "I want to go back and talk to that kid as soon as we finish here" Courtney stated matter-of-factly as she counted the number of ampules of digoxin.

Dot was a little surprised. "What for?" she asked. "He's gonna be all right. Everything's been done for him, but the Psychiatric consult and they'll do that once he gets admitted to a room upstairs."

"I know. I just can't help wondering why he did it. He seems like a really nice kid. I feel sorry for him."

"Let me tell you something, Quinn," Dot began in her seasoned and experienced "nurse" voice. "I don't understand people who try to commit suicide. If you really want to die, there are plenty of effective ways of doing it. Swallowing a bunch of sleeping pills when you know someone is due to come home in the next ten minutes and will surely find you and save you, turns my stomach. It's a waste of my time. If you wanna die, fine. Die. But do it right. Don't waste valuable time that I could be using to help people who really want to live. This 'cry for attention' stuff just turns me right off."

"I don't see it that way, Dot" Courtney said in all sincerity. I think it's sad that anyone, especially a sixteen year old, feels he has no other way to communicate or to ask for help without taking such a big risk. You know, we rushed him in here, pumped his stomach, gave him the finest medical care available, but no one, including myself, ever took the time to talk to the kid. We just judged him as some kind of a nut, did our job and now are just waiting to push him off on the Psychiatrists. I don't think I'd want to be treated that way."

Dot saw nothing wrong with the patient's treatment. "Why not?" she asked. ""He's alive to tell his story, isn't he? Let him tell it to the shrinks. I, for one, just really don't want to hear it. I don't even have **time** to hear it."

"I think we should make the time, before we're so quick to just label him a nutcase and blow him off to Psychiatry. He's just a kid. He might be really embarrassed right now. Or remorseful. I think he needs to know that someone is willing to listen. And not just when he gets on the psych floor."

"You're wasting your time, Quinn. You'll see. You better toughen up and get used to taking care of the priorities."

"Treating this kid like a human being **is** a priority."

"Suit yourself Quinn. The world is full of misery and frustration. No one gets away scott-free. But you don't have to make things worse by trying to kill yourself. And if you do, you should at least be considerate enough not to inconvenience other people with it. Do it right, if you're gonna do it, and don't bother me with the dramatics."

Courtney could see she was not going to get her point across to Dot. Dot was a great nurse, but everyone has shortcomings, and this, Courtney supposed was Dot's only shortcoming as a nurse. Courtney saw having a respectful and sincere talk with the boy as one of the most important interventions on her part.

O.K., of course the medical part came first, but that didn't mean that supporting him emotionally wasn't every bit as important. It was why Courtney had become a nurse. It was one of the most important parts of her job. Yet, there was no accurate way to describe it. She had to laugh when she thought about the cost of a code or of medication, or of just opening the code cart. All of those things were chargeable items. Just ask the insurance companies. Just ask the administrators and the Purchasing Department. But, how do you put a price tag on a few kind words or on a reassuring hand on a frightened and trembling one? How do you explain that your time is well spent, soothing a furrowed brow, or just quietly listening to a tirade of tears? What about explaining to the patient what the doctor just said in terminology that may as well have been a foreign language? And what about answering questions that the patient was either too intimidated or too confused to ask the doctor? This, to Courtney, was what nursing was all about. This was why she had chose it as a profession. The other things were necessary too, but she hated that the nurturing and supportive part of nursing was so grossly overlooked and underrated.

They finished restocking the cart and things seemed to be under control for the moment. "I'll be in with that kid if you need me for anything, Dot" Courtney said, "but before I go, there's something I want to ask you."

"Shoot" said Dot, as she put a new seal on the cart that marked it as ready for the next emergency.

"You're in love with Mike Murphy, aren't you?"

Dot was speechless. Caught completely off guard. Her hands were frozen on the last drawer she had closed and her eyes remained on the seal she had just applied to the cart.

"Am I that transparent?" she finally asked.

"Not really. It took me a while to figure it out." Courtney answered.

"I've been in love with him for a very long time" she said it almost sadly.

"He's too blind to see it. If he's too blind to see it, I don't exactly feel real confident about telling him."

"What's this?" Courtney asked. "The most confident person I know is feeling insecure?"

"Look Quinn, it's fine the way it is" Dot said almost gruffy. "We have a good friendship going for a lot of years. Maybe that's the best you can ask for."

Courtney spoke softly. "Believe me, it's not. It can be so much better. I know because I had it once. And my husband started out as my friend at first and it only got better and better from there on in. Everyone deserves a least a chance at that."

Dot smiled. "Well, who knows. Maybe some day I'll work up the nerve to let him know."

Chapter Nineteen

"Dr. Numb Nuts"

"Nine-One-One sounds good to me," Dot said to Courtney as they gave report to the next shift and had most of their patients transferred to the appropriate floors.

"Sounds good to me too" said Courtney distractedly, as she finished counting the narcotics in the cabinet and made sure everything they had used had been signed for.

"Besides, I want to hear how your little talk with the "attempted suicide" went."

"Yeah and I want to hear more about you and this Mike Murphy story" Courtney added. "And speaking of Mike Murphy, how'd that guy make out in the OR? The 'murder suspect'. Have you heard anything?"

"First of all, technically he's not a murder suspect. Mike and I and now maybe Dennis, the husband, are the only ones who **really** suspect him of Devon's murder. But I'm not usually wrong about these things - and neither is Mike."

"So what's gonna happen to him when he gets out of the OR and goes to the floor? Are they going to post a police guard at least?"

"They can't really do that yet. Mike says they don't have enough real evidence to hold him. And even though he's got O+ blood, which is the same type that was found from the scrapings under Devon's fingernails that night, he's still not considered a murder suspect. Half the people in the world have O+ blood."

"What about the parents of the children?' Courtney asked. "Was he able to get them to press charges?"

"Nope." Dot was almost nonchalant. "Of course, technically Mike could press charges since he witnessed the whole thing, but he really doesn't want to go against the wishes of the parents and drag those two kids through any more than they've already been through."

"So what happens next?" Courtney was sincerely concerned.

"The police will question him while he's in the hospital here, and they'll ask the nurses on the floor to inform them when he's ready for discharge. That way they can arrest him if they've got enough evidence by then, and at the very least, they can keep a close eye on where he goes and what he does."

Courtney grabbed her purse and jacket, "C'mon" she said, "let's get to Nine-One-One. We have a lot to discuss."

But J.J. called to them from cubicle five, just as they were about to make their escape. "Courtney, Dot! One of you guys want to give me a hand, please? I know you're on your way home, but honest, it'll only take a minute."

"I've heard that story before" Dot answered knowingly.

"No, really, Dot" J.J. was almost pleading. "I'm trying to put in a subclavian line (an I.V. into a large vein that runs just below the collar bone). I know you guys are off duty, but it'll really only take a minute if one of you can give me a hand."

Both nurses knew J.J. most definitely was hoping for Courtney to volunteer. That's why Dot stepped in and saved the day for Courtney and frustrated J.J. further.

"O.K., I'll do it" said Dot, "but you owe me one after this" she said conditionally.

"Sure, anything. I'll buy you a drink down at Nine-One-One when I get off duty" he said cheerily. "That's where you're headed isn't it?"

"That's where we **were** headed" said Dot, as she removed her jacked and resigned herself to staying another good twenty minutes or half hour. She turned to Courtney and said, "You go on without me. I'll be there as soon as J.J. finishes. Maybe sooner" she added with a grin.

Courtney heard Dot lecturing J.J. about never bothering a nurse when she's off duty again. Their voices faded as they entered cubicle five and Dot was saying "I don't **care** that there was no one else around to ask. That's your problem. Next time, ask someone who cares."

Courtney made her way out the door into the soft Spring night. The air was musky and salty and the dogwood trees in front of the hospital were in bloom. Sure signs of Spring. Soon the Summer crowds would be down and the Emergency Room would look like a clearance sale at Macy's During the Summer, the population along the Jersey Shore seems to triple. Everyone would be in a party mood and the boardwalk and beaches and summer houses would be filled to capacity with college kids and Philadelphia "yuppies". Sometimes, especially on weekends, it looked as if the entire population of New Jersey moved to the far east perimeter of the State to escape the inland heat. If the State of New Jersey were a ship, surely it would tilt to one side during the weeks between Memorial Day and Labor Day.

Courtney liked to see it coming though, even though it meant much busier nights at work. It was electrifying to see the summer cottages and houses finally revealed after having been boarded up for the winter. It was lovely to stroll along the boardwalk among throngs of tan and smiling people who were as scantily clad as law would permit. Even the old hot-dog vendors and ice cream stands lent a certain charm to the town. Flocks of seagulls came to life again as more and more fishing boats made their way out into the ocean throwing chum and enticing the winter-gaunt seagulls. Even the birds and ducks who flew south for the winter were beginning to return in the Spring and added further life and sparkle to the ambiance of the Shore in the Summer.

Sometimes, not often, but sometimes, Courtney thought she felt the first stirrings of her old self coming back to life. Of course, she could **never** be her old self again. That was a person she had been before her life and her happiness had been shattered by the pull of a trigger in tr ɔ hands of a drunk. But she had made it through more than a year now, and sometimes now, she could get so involved with her job in the emergency Room, or with reading all the material she needed to read to keep on top of things professionally, that she actually had times when she could go without obsessing about Paul and what things would have been like if he were still alive. She was beginning to accept that Paul was not alive any more and though a part of her had died when he did, part of her had also remained alive. And she knew she had to nurture and protect that part of herself, no matter how small a part it was. It was her only hope. Her only way to go on. Statistically she had a lot more years to live and if she was going to live them, then she wanted to live them being happy, not miserable. Not regretting the past. Not wishing for things she knew could never be hers again. No. She had to nurture that little part of herself that had survived the massive explosion in her heart and teach it to live again. To laugh again. And maybe even to hope again. Her life would have to be different now, but that didn't necessarily mean it couldn't be happy again. In a different way maybe, but she had to believe life could eventually be happy again.

She thought about the sixteen year old suicide attempt tonight. Courtney Quinn understood the feeling of a death wish, no matter how transient that feeling was. She knew first hand that life was anything but kind, and how easy it is for life to devastate you, even when you're all grown up and supposedly able to handle the curve balls that get thrown to you. But even big, strong, well adjusted adults get knocked down every now and then, so certainly, a teenage boy, like the one she had seen tonight was allowed to want to give up for a fleeting moment or two.

She was so glad she had sensed that this was not a "Nutcase" but rather a boy who was confused and needed some understanding, not harsh judgements or damaging labels. She was glad she took the time to pull up a chair and sit down next to him and tell him that he was going to be all right and that if he wanted to talk about it or tell her why he attempted to take his life, she had all the time in the world to listen. She cared and she wanted him to know that.

Up until then, the boy had been very cooperative and polite, but completely unemotional. As soon as Courtney gave him the chance to tell his story, it burst out of him as though he'd been holding it in for a very long time.

His name was Mark and his father had died a year ago. Mark had three older brothers all of whom were married and living locally. Mark, being still in high school, lived with his mother. Mark sorely missed his father and was still grieving his death and feeling that he was too young to have been cheated out of a father, a father whom he had loved deeply and respected immensely.

Mark's mother was not coping well with the loss of her husband either. She began to expect things of Mark that his father had not expected. She imposed strict curfews on the boy and if he were even ten minutes late for one of his curfews, his mother would chastise him and tell him how disappointed in him his father would be. She beat him up with something worse than a club. She beat him with guilt. Then she began to expect bizarre and eccentric things of him. Certainly Mark had expected to play the role of the "man of the house" now, but by his mother's definition that began to take on strange meaning. At first she expected him to sleep in his father's place in the bed with her. Mark knew she was having trouble adjusting and he also knew that any time he defied her, she beat him to death with lines like "Your father would want it this way. He'd expect you to take care of your mother". Soon Mark found it impossible to endure the guilt of not bowing to his mother's every wish. But then things got really weird. His mother expected Mark to have sex with her since his father was no longer there to perform this husbandly duty.

That's when Mark caved in. He couldn't take the guilt of obliging her. And he couldn't take the guilt of not obliging her. That's when he decided that the only way out was through a bottle of sleeping pills that were in the top drawer of his mother's night stand. He didn't care any more. He was too ashamed and embarrassed to talk to his older brothers. He felt terribly alone in the world. He didn't know what else to do.

So when Courtney pulled up a chair and offered in a kind voice, to listen, Mark could no longer resist the yearning for an understanding and compassionate ear. He poured out the whole sordid story along with a store house of tears that he had tried too long to hold in, "like a man".

Mark cried for a long time this evening. He cried because he missed his father. He cried because he was terribly hurt and confused and guilt-ridden by his mother. And he cried because he was afraid that he had been a terrible disappointment to everyone.

Courtney had sat there and listened and soothed and spoke to Mark in a soft and understanding voice. She could almost taste his pain and his shame. And now he was even more ashamed that he had tried to commit the ultimate cowardly act . . . and had failed miserably. She spoke to him in a low and calming voice. She told him he didn't have to be afraid any more. That the situation would be straightened out now. That none of this was his fault.

She was glad when Dot stuck her head through the opening in the curtain and told Courtney that it would be another half hour before the floor would be ready to accept the patient and that he would have to wait here, in cubicle eight, until they were ready. Courtney wiped Mark's face with a cool washcloth, being very careful not to disturb the tube that had been put through his nose and reached into his stomach to empty the contents.

She told mark that she knew how badly he was hurting right now. She told him she knew what the pain of losing someone you loved so much was like. And he knew she wasn't lying. He could tell they were comrades. She began to tell him an odd story about how they test patients to assess their level of consciousness sometimes. At first he didn't understand why she was telling him this, but then it began to dawn on him. She told him that when someone seems to be unconscious and doesn't respond to people talking to them or touching them, they then test for a response to "deep pain". The nurses and/or doctors do this by pinching the skin very hard in the center of the chest. This is a last resort for trying to ascertain a person's level of consciousness. Courtney told Mark that after her husband died, she used to watch the doctors do that to patients and she used to think that even though that was the deepest kind of pain they could inflict on a person with any level of consciousness, it seemed like nothing compared to the kind of pain she was feeling in her heart.

Mark understood then. He realized that this nurse knew something about the kind of pain that he was feeling. He knew that he was not the only one in the world who had hurt so badly. And most importantly, he looked at Courtney, so alive, so compassionate and giving and realized that it must be possible to survive this kind of pain. He was beginning to feel better. He was beginning to be determined to make a go of it like this young nurse had. He could see the light at the end of the tunnel .. . . and he was drawn to it. Now he was willing to pay the price for his actions. If she could do it, then so could he. And he would do whatever it was going to take to straighten his life out again. He believed her when she told him that there were people here who would help him. He was ready to accept that help now.

At that moment, two of Mark's older brothers came rushing in and hugged their little brother and told him they had no idea what he had been going through. They each offered to share their homes with him and to get their mother the help she obviously needed.

Courtney left then. She wasn't needed there anymore. She could see that Mark was going to receive a lot of help from at least his two brothers. He would be O.K. She was certain of it. And then she noticed an odd feeling that she never would have guessed was possible. For some reason, her own pain seemed to have lifted somewhat.

She took a deep breath through her nose of the aromatic Spring night, trying to separate and appreciate all the separate scents of Spring. But they all came together in a lovely combination of fragrances and hues. And suddenly she didn't want to separate them. She realized that it was the combinations of new grass and salt air and dogwood trees that made for such a sweet and lovely incense. She thought, for the first time, that maybe she shouldn't keep separating the events of her life into good and bad categories. Maybe she should just take them all in as they happened and make the most of what that left her. It was time to live again.

. . . .

When she got to Nine-One-One, the usual crowd was there. She patted Boris, Frank Stoner's Rotweiler, on the head as she passed him and she took a seat at the bar between Jeff Allen (Fred Gantz's new partner) and the Padre.

She was chatting amiably with Jeff and Fred. The Padre was keeping his ever watchful eye on Mike Murphy, whose judgement, no one trusted these days, especially since they knew the guy Mike suspected of murdering his daughter lay helpless in a hospital bed right now. But, all heads turned as the angry voice of So What, Dot and the apologetic voice of Joseph James, III, D.O. floated through the air, even before they opened the door to enter the tavern. Everyone already knew they wouldn't want to be in J.J.'s shoes.

"I don't care how stressed you were!" shouted So What, Dot. "The least you could have done was let me know he was an AIDS patient so I could at least protect myself. . . from the both of you!"

"Dot, I'm really sorry! How many times do I have to say it?" J.J. pleaded as the door swung open and Dot entered in a huff.

"Whoa!" said the Padre as Dot grabbed a stool and J.J. grabbed the one right next to her. "What's all the commotion about?" asked the Padre in a clerical voice.

"Give her anything she wants" said J.J. to Sam Manetti, the bartender.

"What I want is your ass .. .. ..in a courtroom!" asserted Dot.

The Padre didn't like fights. Especially fights among people who were his friends. People who had been good friends themselves. "Will one of you please tell us what's going on?" persisted the good Padre. "I'm sure it's something we can clear up."

"Yeah, we can clear it up all right around the same time someone figures out how to 'clear up' a little case of AIDS!" Dot would not be placated.

"Well, for Chrissake, somebody tell us what happened!" demanded Mike Murphy.

"I'll tell ya what happened" chortled So What, Dot. "Numb Nuts over here" she said raising her beer mug to J.J. "talked me into staying overtime to help him put in a subclavian line. That wasn't bad enough. I don't mind doin' the guy a favor, Ya know? But he forgets one teensy little thing. He forgets to tell me that it's an AIDS patient whose chest we're diggin' through like a bulldozer, looking for the subclavian vein."

J.J. had already accepted that he was never going to get a chance to say anything in his defense, so he just sat there miserably sipping on his beer. His goose was cooked.

"Well ain't you supposed to treat **all** patients like they got AIDS, just in case?" asked Mike Murphy.

Dot was ready for that one. "Yeah. And I did. Only problem is that 'Numb Nuts' here, goes to hand me the needle he was using to dig for the vein, only he doesn't look at what he's doing and he puts the needle in my hand all right . . . right through the glove!"

There was a gasp heard all around the bar and J.J. wished Dot would quit calling him "Numb Nuts". It made him uncomfortable. And it made him afraid that speaking of his genitals so casually, might give Dot some crazy ideas for revenge.

"It's really no big deal" Dot went on. "Just ask J.J. It just means that now I've been exposed to the AIDS virus. At the worst I might die. And at the least, I have to have my blood tested every six months for the rest of my life. But, hey, just buy me a drink and give me a heartfelt apology and we'll call it finished business, J.J.. No problem." Sarcasm was dripping from her voice and Maalox was dripping from J.J.'s lips in bigger amounts than usual.

Dot was not bashful about getting up and walking around the bar to show everyone the rather significant needle prick in the palm of her hand. She even made J.J. look at it again when it was his turn. When she got to Mike Murphy, he moved down a stool and patted the seat of the stool next to him for her to sit down. She took him up on his offer, but was too miserable to appreciate the significance of Mike Murphy making such a friendly gesture.

Everyone bought Dot drinks that night. Even Stoner the Loner. He sent Boris prancing up to the bar with a couple of bucks in his powerful jaws and he laid them obediently on the bar, nodded his big Rotweiler eyes toward So What, Dot and gave an obligatory bark. Then he pranced back to his owner sitting in his usual southwest corner of the bar by himself.

Fred Gantz, who was feeling rather cocky these days since he was no longer the "rookie" among this group any more, and wanting desperately to show off for his new partner scraped his bar stool across the floor as he got up and pulled out his pen knife. He sauntered over to the wall behind Stoner the Loner and carved a notch in the wall above his head. That made eight rounds of beer Frank Stoner had bought in countless visits to Nine-One-One.

Courtney Quinn was the only one who knew the night had not been a total loss for Dot McFadden as she sat across the bar and watched Dot and Mike Murphy talking like the two old friends that they were .. .. ..and like the two new lovebirds they just might become.

Chapter Twenty

Taking Chances

Courtney was just finishing up restocking the code cart for the third time so far this evening. It had been a busier than usual evening, a sure sign of the fast approaching summer. She felt a presence behind her and turned to see Brain Willis, one of the two detectives who was working feverishly on the Devon Murphy-Donahue murder.

"Hello" Courtney smiled pleasantly at him as she placed a new seal on the cart. Brain and his partner, Lou Simon, had been spending a lot of time around the hospital lately. They were usually up on Eight North, the surgical floor, where the assailant of the two children and the possible murderer of Devon Donahue, was a patient, still recovering from his shattered jaw and various and sundry other injuries. Both detectives usually passed through the Emergency Room on their way out.

"Courtney, can I talk to you when you get a free minute?" Brain asked politely.

"Sure" she said, a little confused about what information he could possibly need from her. "Right now's as good a time as any. Of course I can't guarantee what might come flying through those doors, but I'm willing to take a chance if you are."

"Can we go in the back room please?" Brain asked, leaving Courtney unsure if he was just very professional or just very polite. He was a little of both she decided as he stepped back and allowed her to go first.

"Coffee?" she asked, as she poured herself a cup.

"Yes, please" was Brian's answer.

"So, what can I do for you?" Courtney began, thinking how good it felt to sit down for a minute and relax between catastrophes.

"I understand you were working down here the night they brought in Devon Murphy."

"That's right" Courtney said matter-of-factly.

"That was the same night they apparently brought in this bum who's up on the eighth floor right now with a wired jaw. You know the guy. The one Mike Murphy witnessed trying to accost two children."

"I know the one" Courtney answered. "He's the same one you guys think might have murdered Mike's daughter, right?"

"Well, Mike's a lot more sure of that than we are. I mean, we gotta **prove** these things."

"But, there are an awful lot of clues that seem to point to him, don't you think? I mean, I'm no detective or anything, but I remember he came in that night with long, deep fingernail scratches on his arms and neck. A few of them even had to be sutured before we released him. And that earring. Dennis Donahue says that's the other half of the pair he and Devon used to wear. Not to mention the tattoo . . . "

Brain Willis interrupted. "Look, with all due respect, we're well aware of those clues. And yes, they do look suspicious, but it's not enough to hold him on. We're looking for more. Something that will definitely hold up in court. Can you tell me anything, **anything** you remember about him that night."

"Sorry Brain" Courtney answered honestly. "I'm afraid you're talking to the wrong person. Dot McFadden took care of him that night. She and J.J. sutured him up and released him. You'd have to talk to them."

"Yeah, I figured as much, I just don't want to leave any stone unturned. You'd be surprised where some of the most valuable clues turn up sometimes." He took a long sip of his coffee and stared into space.

"Have you been able to get an identity on the guy upstairs yet? Like a name or an address or something?"

"Hah, it's pretty hard to talk when your jaw's wired. Plus he's got a splint on one hand and an I.V. in the other. Plus his eyes are still swollen shut. It's pretty tough to get any information out of him. He can't write and he can't really talk. Funny thing is, it'll probably be just as hard to get him to talk even after his injuries start to heal. He doesn't seem to be the most cooperative guy in the world."

"So he's still a 'John Doe' for the records, huh?" Courtney asked, knowing that any unidentified male patient that came in was automatically called 'John Doe' for the records. Females were called 'Jane Doe'. She wondered who ever came up with those names and what had been the significance of choosing them.

"Yup, still 'John Doe' far as we're all concerned. But if Mike Murphy ever gets to this guy, and I'm afraid he might, his name might as well be 'Dead Meat'."

Courtney laughed, but she knew Brian Willis was serious. Everyone who knew him was afraid of what Mike Murphy might do. Not that anyone blamed him, but no one wanted to see him lose his hard earned and o-so-close pension for taking matters into his own hands.

"We go up and try to talk to the guy almost everyday" Brian continued, "and the nurses are going to notify us the night before the guy's supposed to be discharged, just so we can at least keep an eye on him and keep tryin' to get more solid evidence so we can lock him up."

"The parents of those kids still don't want to press charges, huh?" Courtney asked.

"Nope. We've all tried to talk them into it. Even told them what we suspect him of, even though technically we're not supposed to do that. But it doesn't matter anyway. Those people made up their minds that those kids have gone through enough."

"I guess you can't blame them" Courtney said into her coffee.

There was a short, but tension filled silence before Brian Willis spoke again.

"Courtney, I didn't wanna just ask you about the guy upstairs. I mean I did, but there was something else too."

Courtney couldn't imagine what else it could be. Oh, wait a minute, yes she could.

"I, uh, I know you were married to a cop once and I know you're just coming through a very hard time." Brain was looking down and blushing a little. "And I'll understand it you say 'no', but I was just wondering if you'd like to go out with me sometime."

Courtney smiled. She didn't know what else to do. She didn't know if she was ready for this yet. Of course all her friends and all her relatives and all the psychology books said she should be ready to date again, but her own heart wasn't quite sure. The thought of it frightened her.

"I don't mean going to Nine-One-One or any of that stuff" Brian went on. "I mean a real date. A place where we don't have to run into any cops or hospital people. And we can talk about anything and everything that doesn't have anything to do with crime and hospitals. If you want, that is."

Courtney was scared. She really didn't think she was ready yet. But something in her made her say yes. Call it the healing process. Call it the survival instinct. But call it a date. A fresh start. Brian seemed like a nice enough guy, even though she really didn't know him that well and it would be good to get out, to get away from the daily strain of emergencies and pressures. She couldn't imagine what Brian could possibly be capable of talking about besides police work. That was all she had ever heard him talk about. She hoped he would keep his promise. She just wanted to have fun.

"I'd like that" she heard herself saying.

Brian's face lit up like he'd just solved a murder case. "Great!" he said, a bit boyishly, a bit endearingly. "You look at your schedule and let me know what night is good for you, and I'll work around your schedule." He was actually beaming.

. . .

"Of all the stupid, brainless, dimwitted stunts to pull" roared Mike Murphy as he entered Nine-One-One two nights later. The usual crowd was there, but no one really paid him much mind. They'd heard far worse tirades than this from him and they simply prepared themselves for more of the same. He was still in the beginning stages of a tantrum. Surely it would escalate into a rampage and possibly, if the matter were important enough, into a full blown conniption.

"Mike, Mike, settle down" said the good Padre as Mike headed toward his usual barstool next to the Padre. "What's wrong?"

"What's wrong? What's wrong?" Mike said, repeating the question, finding it hard to believe that the whole world didn't know what was wrong by now. "I'll tell you what's wrong" he exploded. The Nine-One-One patrons braced themselves. "I went up to the eighth floor tonight to see if that slithering bucket of scum was ready to do any talking yet. He wasn't in his bed, so I figured they must of taken him down for an x-ray or something. So I wait around for a bit. Then I realize that his bed is all made up, nice and fresh, like it was ready for the next patient or something."

There were a lot of deep breaths taken around the bar, and very few people seemed able to let them out again until after they'd heard an answer of some sort.

Father Murphy asked the question that was on everyone's mind. "He didn't die, did he?"

"No. Worse." said a disgusted Mike Murphy. Now, as breaths were let out, no one knew what to expect. "He signed out AMA."

Sam Manetti put a cold beer in front of Mike Murphy and Mike drank the whole thing in one, big deliberate swallow. Sam Manetti, nor anyone else for that matter, was not phased. He put another cold one down in front of Mike as though nothing had happened.

"What's 'AMA' mean?" asked the Padre.

"Against Medical Advice" said So What, Dot as she approached Mike and the Padre from across the bar. "It means, the doctors told him he needed to stay, but he left anyway. Against their advice."

"Didn't the nurses notify anyone? Like the cops for instance?" asked Fred Gantz, incredulous that their would-be prisoner had just walked away.

"Of course not" said Mike Murphy, nothing but contempt in his voice. "That's what they were **supposed** to do. Instead, they just tried to talk him into staying and when that didn't work, they notified the intern on call that the guy was leaving AMA. The intern was in the middle of his evening nap or whatever it is they do in those on-call rooms. He just told the nurses to make sure the guy signed the form that releases the hospital of any responsibility. **Everyone** forgot to notify the station, even though it was written all over the Goddamn chart!"

Father Murphy put a consoling arm around his buddy. "Mike, I'm sorry. But mistakes happen. You know that."

"Yeah, well there's gonna be hell to pay for this one" Mike said, as close to tears as anyone would ever see him.

"Mike, you'll find the guy. I know you will" said the Padre. "You'll see, you'll have every cop, every detective, everybody who's anybody out there combing the streets for him. If he's the guy that murdered Devon, I promise you, we'll get him in the end."

Mike was not to be consoled. "How could those cretins have let him go?!" he remarked, obviously referring to the nurses on the eighth floor.

Courtney knew there was no point in letting Mike know how easily those kinds of things happened. She'd seen it happen before a few times. In fact, as she thought about it, she remembered having been responsible for doing the same thing herself once when she worked on Six-South in Philadelphia when she had been overwhelmed and stressed beyond her limits. Thank God it hadn't been a murder suspect she'd forgotten to notify the police on, but just the same, if you ever worked on those swamped and chronically understaffed floors, you would realize that it was an easy mistake to make. She had no intention of telling Mike that, however.

Sam Manetti appeared in front of Mike with a roast beef sandwich as thick as one of Mike's beefy hands. Mike didn't bite into it. He ripped into it in as ferocious a manner as it if were still alive. Then he washed it down with another beer and once his mouth was finally empty enough to speak again, he began complaining about how rare the roast beef had been again.

"What kind of transient do you have working back there tonight?" demanded Mike of Sam.

"Thanks to you, I ain't got no one working back there. I made that sandwich myself. And even if you didn't like it, you got admit, the price was right."

"You're right, Sam" Mike said apologetically. "I shouldn't complain. I'm just at my wits end now. I gotta find that guy and make a rare, beef sandwich outta him."

Now everyone was really nervous. No one had ever heard big Mike Murphy apologize for **anything**. Ever. This was spooky. Either he was really losing it now, or he was just trying to throw them all off guard.

Everyone would have bet a beer on the latter.

Chapter Twenty-One

The Date

"What's this?" Dot called to Courtney as Courtney was in her bedroom getting dressed for their double date. She knew it was the coward's way out when she'd asked Brian if he'd mind double dating with Mike and Dot tonight, but she wasn't used to dating and she wanted to ease back into it slowly. Besides, Mike and Dot had begun seeing each other regularly on a social basis these days and Courtney could think of no one she would feel more comfortable with for this very significant step she was about to take. She couldn't help it. She just wasn't ready to face the jungle of dating again without support.

"Courtney" Dot called louder this time, thinking she hadn't been heard. "What's this advertisement about a 'Traveling Nurse' assignment. You're not thinking of leaving us, are you?'

Dot was in the living room glancing through a nursing journal that Courtney had left opened to an article about something called 'Traveling Nurses'. At the end of the article were advertisements for different companies, each trying to out do themselves with exotic looking locations where nurses could go 'on assignment'.

"I thought it looked interesting" Courtney answered honestly. "I want to read more about it. It might be a possibility someday" she called into the living room. Then she changed the subject to more serious matters. "What do you wear to a place like this? I know nothing about it" she called to Dot.

Dot stepped into the doorway of Courtney's bedroom. "Honestly, Quinn. It's just a date, for God's sake. Just wear whatever makes you feel relaxed. And like dancing. They always have a great band in this place. Real versatile. They play all kinds of music. Even the kind old fogies like me and Mike like."

"I don't mean to be rude Dot, but we've been friends for quite a while now and I don't have any idea how old you are. Is it O.K. for me to ask you that?"

Dot laughed. "Maybe that's <u>why</u> we've been such good friends. I don't dig into your painful past of losing your husband, unless of course you want to talk about it. And you never ask me any of the personal stuff, like my age or how many times I've been married."

Courtney was embarrassed now, but Dot let out an easy laugh. "Just for the record, I'm forty-seven. I was married once when I was just out of high school to a guy who wasn't ready for big time commitments like marriage. We were only kids. We were real unhappy when the pressures of the real world started hitting us. We got divorced after only a year. No kids. I never really wanted to get married again after that. Never trusted my feelings again." She was quiet for a moment. "There. Now you know everything there is to know about Dorothy McFadden" she added.

"I don't think that's true" Courtney said kindly. "I happen to suspect there's a lost more to Dorothy McFadden than meets the eye. Butw thanks for revealing that much. I always wondered about that stuff with you," she giggled.

"So, what about you, Quinn? Is this your first real date since Paul died?" She was playing tit for tat.

"Paul didn't die. He was killed" Courtney corrected her.

"I see." Dot said softly. "Ouch, it still hurts a whole bunch, doesn't it?"

"Yes, it does." Courtney looked at herself in the mirror, still with wet hair from the shower and still wearing her bathrobe. "Oh God, they'll be here soon!" she said looking at the clock. "Dot, what am I supposed to wear?! Help me pick something out!"

"My, aren't we nervous" Dot observed. "Look. This place where we're going is no big deal. It's a hip little joint, even though you may not think Mike and I are capable of being 'hip' at our age. They have a great band, like I told you. There's a little dance floor, and wine bottles with candles in them on the tables. Not very original, but very cozy and very casual. If you get too dressed, you'll stand out like a sore thumb. And we're all off duty tonight. No sore anything." Dot was relaxed and smiling. Courtney hadn't seen her this unwound or soft looking since she'd met her. Amazing what love could do to a person.

"O.K., I'll wear something casual. Something relaxed. I better, because I certainly don't _feel_ relaxed." Courtney answered as Dot went back to the living room to wait for their dates. It had been pre-arranged that Mike and Brian would pick them up at Courtney's place, since she was more centrally located to everyone.

She didn't know why, but Courtney wanted to look really good tonight. Not that she was terribly attracted to Brain or anything. He was a nice guy and all that, but she wasn't trying to impress him. She felt like looking good. Like not looking like a nurse. She wanted to be cool and hip tonight. She wanted to dance and to laugh and to have some fun with good friends.

She pulled on a pair of nice blue jeans. Not too nice, just nice enough for a first date, but casual enough to be "hip". Speaking of hips, she turned around to see her rear view in the mirror. Her android pelvis filled out the narrow cut jeans perfectly. There I go, already, she laughed at herself. Being all "nursie" already. An android pelvis is the kind of narrow pelvis that most men have and very few women are blessed with. Of course it's only a blessing when you're a woman trying to squeeze into a narrow cut of jeans. It stops being a blessing when you're about to give birth. Paul used to always get mixed up on the medical terminology she had tried to teach him. He just said that she had a bottom like a teenage boy. She had laughed when he first said it. She loved the way he described things and she loved that he appreciated little things like that and told her so. He made her laugh at herself for using "nursie" words like "android".

Then she heard the doorbell ring. She knew Dot would get it, but she also knew she'd better shake a leg.

She grabbed a black, lacy, cotton shirt and slid it over her head. It was cut wide across the shoulders and it exposed the creamy skin of her neck and shoulders. She was putting long silver earrings on when Dot stood in the bedroom doorway again and looked her over from head to foot.

"Perfect" she said. "That's the perfect outfit to wear to this place. Now will you please hurry up!" she said as she disappeared out the door and called, "I have two very handsome gentlemen to entertain while we're waiting for you."

Suddenly, Dot's head popped in the doorway again. "On second thought" she said laughingly, "take your time."

Courtney grabbed her black leather jacket and put it on with the sleeves rolled up. She didn't want to go through the ritual of Brian helping her on with her coat. It would feel too much like a date, even though it was. She had to go very slowly. There were only certain steps she could handle right now. She wanted this evening to be as casual and relaxed as possible.

She took one last look in the mirror and decided to add some silver bangle bracelets. Paul had always loved it when she dressed like this. She remembered one night when she dressed like this when they were going to a party . . . and they never made it out the door. Paul had loved the look and they had canceled their plans for the night, trying not to giggle like two teenagers when they'd made the phone call and the phony excuse.

But Paul wasn't there any more to pull her back inside the door like he had that night. She had to start accepting that. Tonight she had a date waiting in the living room with two good friends. Tonight she would go through with her plans to go out and have cocktails and maybe dance a little with some nice people . . . and try to enjoy it.

Zachary looked up at her from the foot of the bed where he watched her with big, knowing, Bassett Hound eyes. She always felt like he knew what she was thinking. She picked up her black leather purse, kissed Zachary good night, and headed into the living room.

. . .

The music surged out onto the street as soon as Brian opened the door for the women. Courtney liked the music and felt secure being with her good friend, Dot, on this, her first real venture into the world of dating again. They chose a corner table, far enough away from the band to enjoy the music and at the same time, not have to shout to be heard. Courtney could tell she was going to like this place. She made a mental note to herself that she was going to have to get out more. There was so much more to the world than Nine-One-One and the hospital.

They all had a round of drinks and once the wine began to infiltrate her head, Courtney began to rock softly to the beat of the happy and upbeat music.

"Shall we dance?" asked Brian politely offering his hand.

Courtney took it without hesitation and let him lead her to the dance floor. Brian was a surprisingly good dancer. She didn't know why that surprised her, but somehow he just didn't look the type, especially when he was questioning witnesses or trying to solve a murder. But all that was behind them tonight. They had all agreed, no hospital and no police talk. Brian and Courtney danced until Courtney signaled over the music, that she'd had enough for awhile.

Brian led her back to their seats. Courtney was flushed and breathless from the exertion. Brian thought she looked beautiful. He'd never seen this exuberant side of her, though he was an excellent judge of people and had always suspected that it was there.

Then the music changed and the band played a slower, quieter number and Dot and Mike got up to dance. Courtney and Brian sipped their drinks and watched. Somehow, one never pictured either one of them as good dancers. But what they saw astonished them. They made the young people on the dance floor look foolish and out of place. Dot and Mike were as unexpectedly graceful as two giant jungle animals that astound you with their sylph like movements.

Courtney sipped at her second glass of wine. "I wish I could dance like that" she said, admiringly.

"You mean you can't?" Brian asked genuinely surprised.

"Not like that" Courtney laughed. "I can keep a beat, but I never learned any of that slow dancing or ballroom dancing or whatever you call it."

"Well then, it's time you learn" said Brian in all seriousness.

"You know how to do that?" Courtney asked, impressed for about the fourth or fifth time that night.

"Sure, it's easy" Brian said, rising from his chair. "C'mon, I'll show you."

Under different circumstances and without the two glasses of wine, Courtney would have been far too inhibited to go along with this. She was having fun and felt relaxed, she wanted to dance in a man's arms again. It would be so nice.

Brian led her to the floor. Courtney started feeling nervous as he put one hand on her hip and delicately held her hand with the other.

"Brian, wait" she protested. "I don't think I'm going to be very good at this. I really have no idea how to do this."

"Who says you have to be good at it?" he laughed. "Just relax and let me lead you."

112

Brian was a marvelous leader, but even so, Courtney couldn't relax. The wine had flooded her brain . . . but not her feet.

"You're doing fine" Brian smiled at her.

"No, I'm not. But thank you for being so kind" she smiled up at him.

"Still feel uncomfortable?" he asked.

"Very" was her answer.

"Good. I have a great idea. Take your shoes off."

"What?" she said, thinking she'd heard wrong.

But he continued to goad her. He was laughing and she noticed the little crinkles around his eyes when he laughed. He guided her to the edge of the dance floor where their table was. "Take off your shoes" he ordered laughingly.

"Well, I don't want to get arrested for resisting the orders of a law enforcement officer" she said, trying to keep a straight face. She removed her shoes and asked, "Now what?"

"Now step up onto my feet" he instructed.

"You don't have to _tell_ me to do that" Courtney laughed. "I think I've done it a few times already without you having to tell me to."

"No, really. Step up onto my feet. Quick. I like this song they're playing" Brian said seriously.

Courtney looked up into his smiling and encouraging face and threw inhibition to the wind. The tops of his shoes were cool and slippery beneath her stocking feet. Brian smiled a boyish grin and Courtney held on tightly. He swirled her around the dance floor in perfect harmony with the music. The music, Brian, Courtney, they were all one. Courtney felt like a princess, a movie star, a little girl as Brian spun her and dipped and waltzed. Courtney Quinn hadn't felt this free or this happy in a very long time.

The music finished and the band took a break. The four friends returned to their table and Brian pulled one of Courtney's feet to his lap as he gently placed her shoe on it. Then he pulled the other foot onto his lap and did the same. They drank more wine and they all talked and laughed and for a few precious moments, life was no longer cruel or hurtful or serious for any of them.

Brian dropped Mike and Dot off together at Dot's car which was parked in front of Courtney's apartment. Brian and Courtney watched them drive off together and Brian smiled as he watched them fade from sight. "I'm really glad those two finally got together," he said. "They're really good for one another."

This was the part of the date Courtney feared most. The part where she had to decide whether of not to invite Brian in. But she'd had such a lovely time, and she didn't feel like being alone just yet.

"Coffee?" she suggested.

"Sure" Brian answered. "I know a great little place not too far from here" he offered.

He certainly was endearing. "No" she said quietly. "I meant why don't you come in and I'll make us some."

Brian made himself at home in the living room while Courtney fussed around in the kitchen. He noticed the same article that lay on the coffee table that Dot had noticed. The one about "Traveling Nurses".

"You thinking about doing this traveling nurse thing?" he called into the kitchen.

Courtney came out carrying a tray with mugs of coffee and all the accoutrements they would need. "I've been thinking about it" Courtney answered.

"Tell me about it." Brian said. "What's it all about?'

"Well, apparently you sign up with one or more of these companies and you tell them what city you want to go to. They then get you a six to thirteen week assignment in one of the local hospitals and set you up in an apartment, rent free. Then when you finish the assignment, you tell them which city you'd like to go to next and they do the same thing."

"Sounds like a good deal" Brian said, obviously impressed. "What's the catch?"

"Well, for one thing, you tend to spend your life living out of a suitcase and for another, you usually get stuck in the hospitals that are the **most** desperate for nurses, since this is a pretty expensive deal for the hospital. They have to be desperate for staffing. So that means you might end up working in some pretty 'hell holes', if you'll pardon the expression.

"Sounds like a great way to see the country though" Brian offered encouragingly.

"Yeah, I've been seriously thinking about it. I'd like to go some place that never has winter. California or Florida. You know, something like that."

"Want some advice?" Brian asked seriously.

"Only if it's free" she said with a smile.

"Take California. It's a better life out there. Better money. Better attitude. Trust me."

"I do" Courtney said seriously.

Brian looked at her for just a moment, then touched her lips ever so lightly with a gentle kiss. It was followed by a somewhat uncomfortable silence. "Well, now you went and did it" Brian said in a tone of voice that threw her off guard.

"What? What did I do?" she asked, unable to imagine what he was talking about.

"We promised no shop talk tonight and so far, we've had a perfect record. And now, here we are talking about this traveling nurse thing. It's all your fault."

"You started it" she said playfully, glad that he didn't intend to push the kiss any further.

"Yeah, yeah, but it was about nursing, just the same." He said teasingly. "That means I get to ask a 'cop' question now."

"Oh, it does?"

"Yeah, it does."

"O.K., so what's your 'cop' question?" she asked, totally amused and charmed by this man.

"How hard is it for a guy with a wired jaw to take the wires off himself?"

Courtney realized that of course Brian was talking about the patient who Mike suspected of murdering his daughter. The patient who had left the hospital, against medical advice, still with his jaw wired. "It's not very hard, I'm afraid to say" Courtney answered. "He's probably got them cut already so he can talk more normally. We always keep a pair of scissors taped above the bed of a patient with wired jaws."

"You do? What for?"

"In case they vomit or have trouble breathing and we need quick access to getting a tube down their throat. It's really very easy to do. Just a little snip on either side and the patient is able to open their jaw just like before. I'm sure our friend has cut his wires by now."

"Damn" said Brian. "I was thinking all night how it might not be too hard to track down a guy whose jaws are wired shut."

"You never stop thinking about that case, do you?" asked Courtney, truly glad that Brian was so concerned and conscientious. She suddenly wanted to kiss him again, but didn't want to give herself away like that.

"You'll find him" she finally said.

Then as if reading her mind, Brian reached over and this time there was nothing light or even gentle about the way he kissed her. And she was glad.

. . .

The telephone must have rung eight times before Courtney picked it up the next morning. It was Dot.

"Well, how'd it go last night?" she wanted to know.

"It went O.K." Courtney answered noncommittally.

"O.K., let me be blunt. Is he still there?"

Courtney was shocked. Horrified. Insulted. "No, he's not still here. He left last night like a perfect gentlemen." Then she thought for a moment. "Well, maybe not **perfect**" she added.

"So, did you have a good time? Tell me. Mike and I have a bet going."

"I'm not even going to get into that" Courtney wisely decided. "Yes, I had a very nice time" She added truthfully.

"So, how do you feel?" Dot wanted to know.

"Guilty."

"Guilty? I thought you said he didn't stay over and I assume that means that nothing went on. What have you got to feel guilty about?"

"Oh, I don't know Dot. I guess I felt guilty because I had too much fun and maybe I shouldn't be having such a good time yet. Maybe it's still too soon after Paul."

"For God's sake, Courtney!" Dot sounded exasperated. "Who put a time limit on how long you're supposed to feel lousy? Listen to your instincts. If they tell you to have fun, then for Chrissake, have some fun, will ya? Besides, it's been over a year now. It's time to take a chance on life again."

"Speaking of taking chances" Courtney said, trying to change the focus from herself, "it only took you almost thirty years to start trusting your feelings again."

"Ooooh. Good one, Quinn. But, I was stupid. I should have listened to my instincts about Mike a long time ago. We both have wasted a lot of good years crying over the past."

"How's he coping with the loss of his daughter these days? Any better?" Courtney asked.

"I don't think so" said Dot, really serious for the first time in this conversation. "He won't rest till **he**, personally, finds this guy, tortures him, them kills him. It really scares me to see him so obsessed. I guess it's understandable though."

Courtney thought for a moment. "Anything's understandable when someone you love dies. Believe me, I know. Now maybe you can try to understand why fun makes me feel guilty."

"Ever hear of 'Humpty Dumpty'?"

Courtney was confused. "Of course. What's that got to do with anything?"

"Well, all the king's horses and all the king's men couldn't put him back together again, remember?"

"Of course I remember. So what?"

"Well, he never met Dot McFadden. I'm gonna help you two put yourselves back together again, no matter what it takes."

"I believe you" said Courtney, totally convinced.

Chapter Twenty-Two

A Different Kind of Justice

Summer on the Jersey Shore had reached it's relished crescendo and the natives were restless. The boardwalk was constantly mobbed at almost any hour of the day or night. The casinos were hopping and the boardwalk vendors were eagerly selling their wares, like little chipmunks storing a nest egg for the far off, but inevitable, winter.

City Hospital's Emergency Room was almost always packed and Courtney Quinn, with one summer already under her belt, was beginning to feel like a seasoned veteran. At long last she felt secure and sure of herself as she expertly triaged patients and made accurate and valuable assessments. She was her own person now in this chaotic hospital world and it felt good. In fact, it felt so good, that Courtney was beginning to think she was ready for another challenge.

She couldn't get the thought of that "Traveling Nurse" deal out of her head these days. She had written away for information and was immediately inundated with applications, information, and pictures and descriptions of exotic assignments that were available. She never went to her mailbox that there wasn't **something** from the Traveling Nurse companies, even written testimonials from other Traveling Nurses who had tried it and claimed it had added a whole new dimension to their lives. That sounded good. Although, Courtney felt happy and confident in her job now, she also felt ready to add a "whole new dimension" to her life.

Even Dot had to admit it sounded like a good experience, if nothing else. But she didn't want to see Courtney leave. They had become unlikely, but very good friends. And because they were such good friends, Dot could see that Courtney was changing from day to day now. She was becoming stronger and more willing to take chances. She'd been dating Brian for most of the Summer so far, and even seemed to be handling that pretty well, even though it was obvious that she had no real romantic ties to him. Of course, Brian would have given his eyes and teeth to keep Courtney here in Atlantic City, if he thought it would do any good. But Brian wasn't a detective for nothing. He knew he was falling in love with Courtney Quinn and he knew she wasn't falling in love with him. He couldn't help but laugh at the irony of how people always seemed to want what they can't have and how they never seem to want the things they can have. Life was funny like that. Ha, ha.

All things considered, it was sort of a frustrating summer for Brian Willis. They still hadn't caught the guy who had murdered Devon Murphy-Donahue.

And though Brian knew Mike would never recover from the loss of his daughter, he was hoping Courtney Quinn would recover from the loss of her husband and suddenly fall madly and passionately in love with Brian. Thank God for the mind's ability to fantasize. Otherwise, there would be no optimism whatsoever in Brian's life these days.

But he and Courtney remained friends throughout the Summer and, for lack of a better word to describe their relationship, they "dated". They met frequently down at Nine-One-One after getting off duty and usually they sat next to Dot and Mike.

Having a romance with So What, Dot had been a good thing for Mike Murphy, maybe the only good thing that had happened to him these days. They sat with each other every night in Nine-One-One and some people, especially Sam Manetti, the owner and bartender, had noticed a definite decrease in Mike's alcohol consumption. Good thing, considering the almost inhuman amounts of Jack Daniels he had consumed during those first torturous months following Devon's death. Most people, especially the Padre, felt certain it was Dot's strong personality and undying devotion to Mike that had been such a good influence on him and that seemed to be pulling him through. In fact, come to think of it, Mike hadn't even had a fight with the cook, or anyone else for that matter, in a couple of weeks now. Maybe there was hope.

It was another steamy, sultry July night when the 3 to 11 crowd at the hospital lethargically dragged their weary bones into Nine-One-One. And in just another hour, Sam would see the four to twelve shift of cops come sauntering in. The whole scene was so predictable.

Dot, Courtney and J.J. arrived together. J.J. seemed to have brought a fourth person along to join them. Sam had never seen her before, but she looked young and innocent. Just the type J.J. liked because she was just the type he could impress with his red Corvette and the "M.D." tags. Sam wondered if maybe he should proof her, she did look awfully young. Then he thought maybe he should warn her, since she looked totally taken with J.J.. He decided to do neither. People always had to learn for themselves. That, he knew for sure.

He set everyone up with their usual cold, draft beers and stood at the end of the bar to partake in his favorite pastime: eavesdropping on several conversations at once.

It wasn't long before Mike Murphy showed up and took his usual seat between Dot and the Padre. He was followed shortly by Brian, who took his usual seat beside Courtney. The cold beers were flowing. It was an exceptionally hot and humid night and even the ceiling fans that usually blew the cool ocean air around, were not sufficient tonight. Sweat seemed to glisten on everyone's cheek.

It was the kind of night that cops learn to dread. For some reason, people seem to get a little crazier than usual in this kind of weather, and though everyone in there was off duty at the moment, there was no telling what kind of unexpected disturbance could erupt. There was a foreboding aura in the air.

Sam was the first to sense it. He didn't know why he felt it, but when Mike ordered his "well done" roast beef sandwich, Sam got a chill in the 90 degree heat. He'd just hired a new cook and he didn't know how well he was going to work out. Sam had his own doubts about him, but he also knew that the roast beef had better be well done, or Mike, as well behaved as he had been would be back there jacking him up. The heat did crazy things to people. Sam figured he'd just stroll in the back and tell his new cook to be sure the roast beef for that sandwich was well done.

By some people's standards, it was well done. By Mike Murphy's standards it wasn't. And those were the standards that counted.

"I see you got me eating live animals again" Mike said to Sam around a mountainous chunk of roast beef. "Does your cook speak English this week? Cause I got a few things I'd like to tell him."

"Oh relax, Mike" said So What, Dot. "It doesn't look that bad to me. I'm going to the Ladies Room and when I come back I expect to see you sitting right here eating that sandwich. There's nothing wrong with it."

"That shouldn't be a problem" remarked Mike a little too calmly. "I can probably go back there and beat the snot out of whatever cretin made this sandwich by the time you get back from the Ladies Room."

Dot gave Mike an admonishing look, then headed toward the Ladies Room.

"C'mon, settle down Mike" Sam said as he watched Mike begin to push his cumbersome frame off the barstool. "He's a new cook. Give him a break. I think he did a pretty good job."

"Yeah, it you don't mind a little fresh blood on your sandwich" Mike said in a tone of voice that scared Sam. Mike was about to get into another fight with a cook. Sam was resigned to it. He knew things had been too quiet around here for too long.

Mike was making his way back into the kitchen as Courtney was exiting the Ladies' Room. She threw Brian an "Oh no, not again" look and stayed put so she could hear the goings on back there and maybe signal the others for some help in there in case things got too far out of hand.

"What do you call this?!" thundered Mike as he forcefully swung the kitchen door open with one massive hand while he held the half eaten sandwich in the other. The puny little cook didn't even look up as he went on slicing more of the rare roast beef that Mike had received. Mike walked deliberately over to the frail little cook, putting every ounce of his 225 lb. bulk into each footstep. "I asked you a question, Dimwit" said Mike in his most condescending voice. This time the cook looked up.

He was only about five foot seven and he had to **really** look up make eye contact with Mike's six foot two frame. It was the one move the cook wished he'd never made. Mike's expression of aggravation perceptibly evolved into one of sheer rage as he recognized the still swollen jaw and eyes of the dumb struck, terror-stricken cook. It was **him**. There was no doubt. The murderer of Mike's daughter. Mike didn't care about things like "innocent until proven quilty" or hard evidence or any of that other crap the system would surely throw at him. All Mike cared about was his daughter. His beautiful, beautiful Devon, whose life had been so violently interrupted by this animal. Mike didn't care about pensions or courts of law. All he cared about, all he was capable of, was killing this slimeball.

Courtney thought it was awfully quiet in there for Mike Murphy to have received a rare piece of roast beef. She threw a questioning look across the bar toward Brian and decided to go in and see what was going on. She knew Brian, and maybe even some of the others, would be right on her heels if she needed them. In fact, they'd probably come in even if she didn't need them. She wasn't nervous at all. But she should have been.

As soon as she walked in the door, she saw Mike with his hand around the throat of the cook. She didn't recognize the cook. She thought Mike was over reacting a bit just over a rare roast beef sandwich. "Mike, don't!" she shouted.

Mike was completely taken by surprise to hear a female voice. In his semi-delirious state of rage, he thought it might be the voice of his precious, precious Devon. He turned his head toward Courtney, keeping his grip on the cook's neck. Unfortunately, that gave the cook the only chance he had left. He pulled a knife, probably the same kind he had used on Devon, and quicker than the shot of a gun, he slashed Mike's powerful arm with it, causing Mike to let go momentarily. In a heartbeat, the cook lunged toward Courtney and held the knife to her neck. He pricked a small surface wound into the side of her neck, just to let them know he meant business. He held Courtney with one surprisingly strong yet scrawny arm. Apparently he'd done this before. Mike was across the room, putting pressure on the wound in his forearm that was spurting bright red blood. He felt faint from the loss of blood, but he felt even more resolved to kill this son of a bitch.

It seemed like time had stood still as Courtney felt the warm trickle of blood run down her neck. Where were the others, she wondered. Surely, Brian and the others would be here in a second or two. But no one had made any real noise yet, and it was possible that the others thought everything was under control. No. No, she thought. Brian will come to see. I know he will.

"O.K." said the scrawny cook as he held the knife in his tattooed hand. "Everybody just stay nice and calm and no one will get hurt." He looked evenly at Mike Murphy, who, Courtney knew would never let this guy get away, no matter what. "Just stay where you are, copper and I'll just slip out the door. I'll leave the girl right here in the doorway. No more trouble if everyone cooperates." He began dragging Courtney toward the door and Mike Murphy pulled his gun.

"Oh, no you don't, pal" Mike Murphy said steadily, though his face was pale from the amount of blood he was rapidly losing from the severed artery in his forearm. "I don't know what your name is, but we can find out all that stuff after you're in the morgue. You killed my daughter and now you're gonna pay. You ain't goin' nowhere except straight to hell."

120

Mike raised his revolver and aimed it between the eyes of the scrawny cook. For the first time, it occurred to Courtney that she might possibly die. She looked down at the blood that was now running down her chest from the wound in her neck and all of a sudden, she wanted more desperately than ever to live. She had so much she still wanted to do. Feelings she wanted to feel. A life she wanted to live and maybe even to share. Suddenly it all struck her as very funny. It was so funny to her that now that she finally wanted, really, really **wanted** to live, she just might die. She began laughing. It started off almost as a giggle then ballooned into a raucous, belly laugh. She had never heard herself make sounds like that before. She wasn't even sure it was she, who was making them, they sounded so foreign to her. The man who held the knife to her neck, looked at her as though she were some kind of lunatic. At exactly that moment, a shot rang out and the man dropped the knife and fell, in slow motion it seemed, to the floor.

Suddenly, the little kitchen was filled with everyone who'd been out in the bar. Brian ran to Courtney and held her in strong, protective arms. Jeff Allen and Fred Gantz ran to the cook lying on the floor, guns drawn and aimed at him as he sputtered and begged for his life, not unlike the day they'd had him in a similar position in the ocean. Dot and Sam Manetti ran to Mike and eased him down onto the floor, where Dot began putting pressure on his wounded arm and talking to him in a calm and reassuring voice. Sam yelled out the doorway for someone to call an ambulance.

J.J., not surprisingly, was the last to arrive in the overcrowded little kitchen. Fred and Jeff were still standing over the cook, guns drawn. The man was begging for his life. He had no idea how futile his plea was.

"C'mon Man, don't shoot" he was saying to the hostile faces above him. "I didn't do nothin'. I **certainly** didn't kill that dude's daughter. I don't know what he's talking about."

But Mike Murphy knew what he was talking about and that's all that mattered to anyone in the room.

"C'mon, you gotta help me!" pleaded the man as he lay sprawled on the floor, blood pumping from the gunshot wound that had hit him in the neck. Without some immediate first aid, he obviously didn't have long to live. Maybe he would die before the ambulance got there if no one decided to be compassionate. And no one did.

Four cops, one doctor, two nurses and the tavern owner, sat back and wordlessly watched a man bleed to death right in front of their eyes. There was no need for words. Everyone of them knew what "the system" would do for this man, and no one wanted to give him that chance. It would be their little secret. There would be no need for discussion, no need for any guilt. Everyone in that room was an adult and everyone in that room had made the same choice. Case closed.

The ambulance arrived and the paramedics tended to Mike and Courtney's wounds on the spot. They had to put in a call to the Medical Examiner to come and pronounce a scrawny little man lying on the floor with a knife near his hand, dead. From the looks of things and the stories of the people involved, Mike Murphy had shot him in self defense. Whoever he was.

Epilogue

Sam Manetti had worn his boots to work today. He always wore them when a serious Nor'easter or a hurricane was predicted. Other people would take refuge on the barstools till the tide went out, but Sam Manetti had to walk on the ocean-soaked floors all through the high tide during a storm. Sam was surprised that such a serious storm was predicted this time of the year, even though technically, August was the beginning of "Hurricane Season". Usually they didn't see any kind of severe weather until September. And here it was, only late August and Sam had to drag out his high tide boots already.

But as much as he liked to complain, he didn't mind any of it. He had been the proud owner of Nine-One-One for eighteen years now and he had seen a lot of changes both on the inside and on the outside of those doors. He'd bought Nine-One-One on a wing and a prayer eighteen years ago when the city was in real trouble and was going under fast. That was before the casinos and gambling had been voted in. That was when the area had been nothing but a few little Summer resort towns with small town problems and small town solutions. And he had witnessed the big city problems that had emerged with the advent of all the hotels and casinos. the more things changed though, the more they stayed the same. And that wasn't just on the outside of the tavern.

Some of the biggest changes seemed to occur within the people, especially the people who frequented Nine-One-One. Sitting here every night and watching them was like watching and tasting a little slice of the world. And that's how Sam Manetti liked it. He'd seen enough of the world for himself. Owning and operating Nine-One-One kept him plenty entertained. He broke the golden rule that he had made for himself thirty years ago and decided to have a drink while tending bar tonight and sitting out the storm. He'd have his favorite, while he was at it. Remy Martin. It went down easy. It felt good, especially on a night like this, with the northeast wind whipping cruelly off the whitecaps of the ocean.

He leaned against a corner of the bar and reflected on all that had happened in here of late. He looked at Mike Murphy sitting there next to So What, Dot. What a pair. What a perfect match they were. And to think of all the years Mike had spent crying in his Jack Daniels over his wife who had left him eight, maybe nine years ago. And here, right under his nose for all these years, had sat the ideal woman for him. So What, Dot really loved Mike. Sam had known it for a long time and silently wondered how long it would take for the two of them to realize it. And how much longer it would take for them to admit it.

It seemed odd to Sam that it was only after the biggest tragedy of his life, Mike was able to see clearly enough that Dot was the right one for him. Sam wished them well. He was glad for Mike's happiness now, even though he knew that Mike would be forever changed, forever scarred by the loss of his daughter. Sam knew the feeling only too well, for he had once lost a child too. He didn't have the heart to tell Mike that the pain never stops. Sometimes it's better than others, but it never stops. That's for sure. But at least Mike had the satisfaction of shooting the guy and watching him suffer and die. That had to count for something. That had to have made a small piece of that pain a little more bearable.

And now, here he was, planning to marry So What, Dot. It was going to be a very small and informal ceremony next month. Of course the honors would be performed by the good Padre. Mike and Dot had asked Sam if they could hold the reception afterwards here at Nine-One-One. Well that would certainly be a first. And one that he wouldn't miss for the world.

The most surprising announcement of all that Mike Murphy had made, had nothing to do with his marrying Dot. He had been offered a promotion to Sergeant and this time he had accepted it, much to everybody's astonishment. Maybe old dogs could learn new tricks.

And speaking of old dogs, Frank Stoner or "Stoner the Loner" as he was better known, had finally taught Boris a new trick. He had rigged up a device like the kind you get in the carry-out, fast food places to put soft drinks in. Now Boris could not only trot up to the bar and lay down a few bucks for a couple of beers for him and his partner, but now with this device strapped to his massive neck, Boris was also capable of carrying them back to the table of his master in the southwest corner of the bar.

At the end of the bar, was the good Padre, working as usual, even when it looked like he was just having a friendly beer with Atlantic City's finest. He was sitting next to Jeff Allen tonight and they were looking very intense and talking very seriously. From the bits of conversation Sam could hear as he kept the drinks flowing, Jeff had apparently shot and killed his first criminal and was feeling overwhelming guilty over it, even though he had had no other choice but to shoot to save his own life. Yes sir, the Padre was working hard tonight.

And then there was Courtney Quinn sitting beside her friend Brian Willis. Brian was a very sad friend these days because Courtney had finally made the decision to take one of those Traveling Nurse assignments. California was the State that had won her interest and Sam was certain that there was a whole new life waiting for her out there. So was Brian and that's the reason he was feeling sad these days. He'd had high hopes for a relationship with her. But despite Brian's disappointment in seeing her go, Sam was glad to see that Courtney was finally healed enough to spread her wings and fly again. She always reminded him of a bird with a broken wing and now that bird was whole again and ready to soar. He liked that.

J.J. had decided that younger, less worldly women were more his type - and he must have been right, since, by the look of his lips lately, he'd obviously cut down on the Maalox. Fred Gantz, who was so very happy not to be the "rookie" of the group any more, was sticking close to J.J. and the cute little student nurse he brought in with him as often as possible.

Sam Manetti took another swallow of his Remy Martin and sat back. It went down so easy. It softened the edges of the cruel world. And although alcohol had gotten a bad name over the last few years, Sam had to respect what people had known about alcohol since time began. It certainly had its advantages. In a world where everyone eventually has to face their own demons, booze certainly seemed to soften the hard edges and even slow down the process until a person was truly ready to face a life filled with surprises, many of them disappointing surprises.

He looked around at the crowd before him. They were his little piece of the world. It was a world filled with the bullets of bad guys and good guys. It was a world filled with the bandages and compassion of the kind of people who put other people back together again. And it was a world filled with all kinds of people who sometimes needed the anesthesia that only a good shot of booze could achieve. It was a world of Band-Aids, Bullets and Booze.

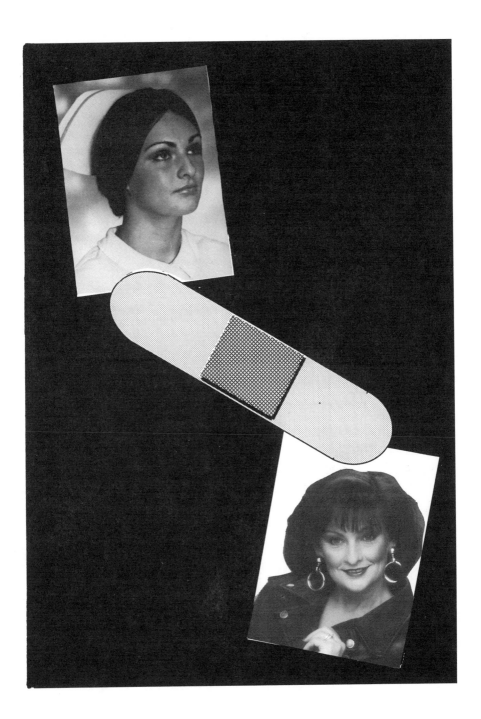